NEW MAPS

deindustrial fiction

VOL. 1, NO. 1
WINTER 2021

LOOSELEAF PUBLISHING

Bayfield, Wisconsin

About *New Maps*

New Maps publishes stories in the growing genre of deindustrial fiction, which explores the long decline of industrial civilization, its aftermath, and the new worlds made possible by its departure. The magazine also publishes essays, book reviews, letters to the editor, and other content that examines these themes. For more on the philosophy of the magazine, see the website below, or get acquainted by way of this issue.

Submissions of any of the foregoing may be addressed to the editor at either of the addresses below. Story submission guidelines may be found on the website or requested by post.

New Maps is published quarterly by Looseleaf Publishing. Subscriptions are currently available in the U.S., Canada, U.K., Ireland, Australia, New Zealand, Belgium, Germany, Norway, and Japan. An annual subscription is $42.00 USD for U.S. addresses, with different prices elsewhere, and may be purchased from the website below, or by writing to request an order form.

Postal correspondence:
Looseleaf Publishing
87095 Valley Road
Bayfield, WI 54814, USA

Online:
www.new-maps.com
editor@new-maps.com

ISSN pending

Image credits:
- — Cover art copyright © 2021 Nathan B. Peltier.
- — Wooden maps (p. 5): Public domain, from Gustav Holm, *Den danske Konebaads-Expedition til Grønlands Østkyst*, 1883, via Wikimedia Commons.
- — Musk ox hunt (p. 5): Public domain, by Qavdlunâq, orig. from Knud Rasmussen, *The Fifth Thule Expedition, 1921-24*, vol. 8, via Maria Ascher (see note, p. 5).
- — *Always Coming Home* cover (p. 8): Copyright © 2001 University of California Press.
- — Horse in field (p. 74): Copyright © 2021 G. Kay Bishop.

Contents

Introduction

Thanks for reading this first issue of *New Maps*. I'm glad you're here, and I'm very happy to be filling the inaugural issue with stories that are all just stunning in their various ways. Taking up the mantle of publishing deindustrial fiction from Joel Caris and his excellent *Into the Ruins*—and more distantly, John Michael Greer's *After Oil* anthologies—has already been a gratifying project, and I've been glad to see many who wrote such wonderful stories in this magazine's forerunner returning to write here.

I plan *New Maps* to be substantially similar to *Into the Ruins*, so those who knew that magazine should feel on familiar ground here. And I'm also interested in exploring ideas of how it may be able to evolve gradually, to be the best magazine it can be for the community of deindustrial fiction writers and readers, however that community might come together through time—in the spirit of adapting to changes in the world. Currently I'm mulling plans for a somewhat expanded essays section, featuring nonfiction contributed by readers on topics of their interest that deal with the deindustrial future and the stories we use to approach it. In whatever ways possible, I also hope for this magazine to help build and foster the community of people who think about the unfolding long decline of the industrial age. We have a letters section, but what else could be useful? I welcome your thoughts. Someday will there be a "deindustrial singles" section in the back pages? It seems unlikely from here, but who can say?

At any rate, I'm excited to be taking on the project of sharing these stories, just as we need them more and more. For some years recently, it's been possible for mainstream observers to make the case that decline was still only a theoretical possibility, if that, and that the future was still bound to proceed along the trajectory of "progress." As of this year, that position is a deal less tenable, and many more than before are abandoning the orthodox view of the future to look for futures that ring truer. I hope they can find those here.

—*Nathanael Bonnell*
Editor

Letters to the Editor

Dear Editor,

I read a young adult post-disaster novel a few years ago where the family had flour, but ran out of the store-bought yeast they normally used to make bread. If memory serves me correctly, they didn't then create sourdough starter (presumably didn't know about it), and instead stopped making bread. Like all good fiction—it got me thinking. What are my "unknown unknowns," and what items/tools/essential knowledge are the things I should be focusing on?

I read of someone who buys cheap pressure cookers (e.g. at garage/yard sales), because when fuel gets short, pressure cookers will be life-saving. John Michael Greer often talks about ham radios as being a valid communication system that doesn't require un-achievable technical know-how to maintain. I'd love to hear what other readers try to salvage from the waste stream, knowing that the items will come back around to being invaluable, and/or skills that they are working to likewise preserve. I realise that this is a potentially long list of items and skills, so perhaps readers have suggested books or other resources which start to tackle this. Maybe someone could review attempts that have already been done towards this end?

Thanks,
Cathryn

Dear Cathryn,

I would love to hear readers' thoughts on this as well. I've seen the topic approached sidelong here and there—Greer has also said, "Learn to brew beer, and Attila the Hun himself will clap you on the back and tell everyone you're all right"—but I don't recall a full-length discussion on what would be particularly useful to preserve.

Meanwhile, with the editor's privilege of responding to you before anyone else gets the chance, I'll mention that something I've been interested in is old-fashioned printing. I haven't yet bought myself a press and fonts, but in my daydreams I'm setting the text of New Maps by hand from a California job case and printing it with a Washington hand press. (This was primitive even by the 1880s.) That would probably require me to give up day jobs and raise subscription prices to $500 a year, but maybe if I get the equipment I can start up a little sideline in printing cards instead, and help preserve a venerable and nearly moribund art. Doing a little letterpress may not directly save anyone's life—though I'm sure if pressed I could concoct a scenario where it would—but passing the knowledge of printing with metal on to an eventual future without laser printer factories may, in the long run, have a real noticeable positive for the community.

☉

Dear Editor,

May I suggest an interesting topic worth including in many post-peak-oil fictions will be the usage of electricity, the smaller and more local infrastructure creating it, and even possible large-scale attitudes toward its usage, and how different the attitudes may be compared with, say, the late 20th century. May I also suggest a possibility that the different regions and countries will prioritize significantly different methods for electrical generation and usage. I believe it would be interesting for future post-globalization and very-late-industrial-age fiction writers to bring into short stories and novels—the cultural differences in attitudes on electricity between countries, regions, even perhaps urban–rural differences. I strongly believe this will make postindustrial fiction more entertaining and am interested in other readers' opinions.

Goodbye, and may I wish everyone involved in starting *New Maps* the best of luck.

David O Rourke

Dear David,

I agree that electricity is pretty frequently overlooked, not only in deindustrial fiction but also in our day-to-day assumptions about what the future will be like. This point has been made forcefully to me by circumstance. In August my partner and I moved to a little cabin on a country backroad, and its only source of power is an ag-ing solar array. Through the summer, this worked okay for us, and we adjusted to life with no refrigeration besides a cooler on the north side of the house. But when the days got shorter, I discovered the little system no longer seemed able to run my computer—a peculiar difficulty in that I was starting up an internet-dependent business (this magazine) at the time! You don't know what you've got till it's gone.

This is a prime example of a way where the future won't look just like the past. With fairly tinker-friendly ways to make a little electricity now well understood, and the information on how to make useful gizmos that'll run on it available with only a little digging, people of the future certainly won't abandon electronics all at once so as to live a lifestyle that tidily resembles the 1700s.

I've read a number of stories where electricity is about as available as it is currently, and a number where it's entirely absent. I don't immediately recall any where people are muddling through intermittent availability and brownouts, even though that's a reality in lots of poorer countries today. How tightly would people try to hold on to that power? Would you see pay-to-plug-in posts popping up? And as you wonder, how would all this be different from place to place? Worth paying attention to.

☉

Have you considered doing longer pieces or serials? I have every issue of *Into the Ruins*; I loved the concept, but read it less and less as they came

out. It seemed that one story in 4 or 5 would appeal to me. Maybe it was because the short story format is too short to develop detailed ideas about a possible future. I've enjoyed Greer's and [James Howard] Kunstler's novels and similar ones, but short stories in this genre tend to turn me off.
    Bob Wise

Dear Bob,
    I have considered that, and you're not the only person who's suggested to me that this magazine might be a good place to revive the old-fashioned serialized novel—some of the 1800s' classics were released a chunk at a time, like A Tale of Two Cities *and* The War of the Worlds, *and so was even as recent a novel as* Fear and Loathing in Las Vegas.*
    As it currently stands, the New Maps *submissions guidelines encourage writers who have a novel to find a publisher who'll publish it as a novel. But I like the idea of serializing, keeping perhaps one novel going at a time, which would still leave space for plenty of good short fiction, and allow the author to retain the right to republish the whole as one book a few months after the last installment. There's even precedent as close to home as* Into the Ruins, *which split Violet Bertelsen's novella* The Ghosts in Little Deer's Grove *across issues 12–13.*
    *Readers, what are your thoughts? Would you be interested in serialized novels here? If you were to subscribe and then find that one of the stories in your first issue was "Part III" of some-*thing, *would you get excited and order the two back issues, or just get annoyed? Let me know!*

☉

Dear Nathanael,
    I sat down to write a letter for *New Maps* today and what I got was a fantasia on the theme of New Maps.
    New maps, new territories, new landscapes. Borders redrawn. Borders dissolved. Resolution and dissolution of old identities and new. The pew benches once carved from ancient oaks get taken back outdoors into the sacred grove. Winter nights reading yellowed magazines by oil lamplight around the potbellied stove. Reading tea leaves and the patterns of coffee grounds in the chipped cup. Tightening up the windows so the wind don't slip in and the heat don't slip out. A gruel of oatmeal for breakfast mixed with stout. The stew pot is in a constant simmer hanging over the fire. New maps collaged from the old blue highways.
    U.S. 32, the hillbilly highway, once pumped fresh blood into the steel towns of Ohio and the car town of Detroit but now the cities are bleeding back out into the hills, and smaller cities and small towns. Folded maps shoved in the back pocket, folded so much, over and over again, the paper starts to tear and break. We put the maps back together with scotch tape to see where we are going.
    Trace the contour of these hills to see where once a river was flowing, way back in the glacial when. Trickle

of the Mill Creek now flows through that ancient river bed where small towns and neighborhoods sprung up in the valley foundations dug into the wetlands. A rooming house full of shadows and tombstones sits on the ancient springs. Faery folk blood mingles in the veins of coal and gold underneath the primordial hills and drips into the blood of the people.

New times require new maps and redrawn lines. The ruins we entered, found in the forest with debris of concrete and steel and fiberglass memories of a once proud people, and still proud even as they are waylaid low. A tarnished halo of broken glass greets me in these ruins of Seven-Elevens and United Dairy Farmers. We rake through the soil of the urban homesteads and uncover Ding Dong and Twinkie wrappers left alone by the worms and set them aside in a special pile. All the old plastic brittle to be put in the walls makes great insulation. Here at the way station of history I don't know which train to catch. So I study the timetable and the new maps and pause to reflect on a possible destination.

Congratulations on the magazine and I'm very much looking forward to traveling these paths and roads with you and the authors whose words fill the pages.

Justin Patrick Moore,
Cincinnati, Ohio
January 10, 2021

☉

New Maps welcomes letters to the editor. Email editor@new-maps.com, with "Letter" or "Letter to the editor" somewhere in the subject line, and sign with your name as you'd like it to be printed. Or write via post, including your name and a note to consider your letter for publication, to Looseleaf Publishing, 87095 Valley Road, Bayfield, WI 58414, USA. Comments for contributors will be forwarded.

ESSAYS & REVIEWS

Some Notes on Cartography and Storytelling

Nathanael Bonnell

There are very few things we can know for certain about the future, but one of them is that it won't look quite like the present or the past. That's true, of course, of the simple physical aspects of how we and other creatures will live on this planet—from the large strokes such as the obsolescence of fossil fuels and the consequences of the planetwide climate rejiggering now beginning, to the small things like what technologies we'll be able to entertain ourselves with on the long evenings around the winter solstice. But it's also true of the mental and cultural worlds that we and our inheritors will inhabit.

In the year that we've just said a collectively relieved and yet wary farewell to, we've had a blaring and fast-moving example of the rearrangement of the emotional maps of more or less the entire world. A great deal of territory, most obviously, has been claimed by new fears. But cautious gains have been made on the front of self-determination, as some people stay home, figure out how to scrape by, bake a few loaves of bread, catch up on projects they've been putting off for years, and perhaps come to the conclusion that their jobs sucked anyhow. There's also been some push into stillness and meditativeness as the things that filled our days with hustle have sloughed away. And so on: the changes wrought by the present pandemic and our haphazard reactions to it have remade, among other things, our definition of personal space, our trust in supply chains, our attitudes toward gardening, and our music. (In November I heard a charming song in which the narrator gets all dressed up in his green suit, and his partner in her red dress, and they meet at their dining table.)

Certainly, 2020 was one of those years that are mentioned in history books, and some rearrangement of our attitudes is to be expected. But this sort of thing is really happening all the time, at a slower and perhaps more inexorable pace. To take one wide-scale example: having lived a Statesider hailing from the tail end of the '80s, and having known only a government that presents itself as something like an irresistible and faceless force majeure, I could almost find the hippie war protestors of the 1960s charmingly naive—if not for the fact that they seem to have actually helped end a war. Within a couple decades after that fact, though, the government was transformed, from a somewhat approachable collection of human beings who respond to reason and righteous outrage, into

a monolith. Readers from different times and places can doubtless supply con-
trasts of their own between the present and times in their living memory; as
they say, "the past is a foreign country: they do things differently there." And
if changes as considerable as 2020's have come in a single year in which our
material circumstances have stayed mostly the same except for the addition of
one novel pathogen, the cultural and mental changes between this moment and
whatever year the last oil derrick finally stops nodding will amount to an almost
entirely different world. We will be someone else's foreign country, and they are
our *terra* irremediably *incognita*.

To really show the vastness of the difference that can exist between two different times, though, I think it will be useful to dig into a little ethnography. The
difference between two times is, eventually, much like the difference between two
places. And a few examples show that at sufficient distance it's not enough just
to redraw the borders on a map, but it becomes necessary to entirely reimagine
what a map even is.

In the 1880s, Danish explorer Gustav Holm paid a visit to Ammassalik Island
on the craggy east coast of Greenland, and there met a village of Tunumiit Inuit.
He wintered with them, and gathered notes from them about parts of the coast
he hadn't visited. After a while, one Tunumiit man presented him with a set of
maps of the coastline a little further down. They consisted of flattened pieces
of wood, with deep grooves and teeth carved into them to represent the inlets,
points, and islands along that stretch of coast. He mentioned that maps like that
were often made to acquaint people with coastline they hadn't visited, or to tell
stories where the characters' locations and changing viewpoints of the land were
important.[1]

If this seems like an unnecessary length to go to in order to tell a story, it's
worth knowing that in the Inuit language family, orientation to places is a very
exacting and constantly practiced science: where English has *here* and *there*, the
Inuit system has fully eighty words, and there is no way to say simply "there"
without specifying who it's *there* relative to; whether it's up, down, or over *there*;
whether the shape of *there* is roundish or longish; and how the thing that's *there*
is or isn't moving. Likewise, the stretch of coastline represented on the carving is
apparently curvier than the medium allowed the carver to show, but here again
we have to understand that the old Inuit way of understanding space is very
different from the Western one. A different visitor some decades ago handed
some photographs to his Inuit hosts, and found it strange that they looked at
them without turning them to orient "down" toward them. It transpired that the
Inuit, including the kids, also found *him* a bit loopy and possibly slow-witted

---

[1] Harmsen, Hans: "Greenland's Hand-Sized Wooden Maps Were Used for Storytelling, Not
Navigation." *Atlas Obscura*, May 2, 2018. <bit.ly/2VR8CfW>

Ammassalik wooden maps.   Drawing of a musk ox hunt.

for always turning pictures a certain way before looking at them, and that when they put pictures up on their walls, they tacked them happily any which way, with no impediment to understanding them. Drawings from 1920s Inuit are a Cubist-postmodern mindwarp of shifting horizon lines and perspectives, all invented without benefit of Western art schools.[2]

I've dwelt on the subject of the Inuit not because they're uniquely unusual, but mostly because I have some visual evidence I can show to make the point clearer. In fact cultures around the world, especially before the great homogenizing influence of globalization claimed ascendancy, have maintained very different spatial worlds for probably as long as humans have organized themselves into different cultures. Australia, for whatever reasons, is particularly rich with highly non-Western ways of understanding space. Among the Thaayorre of the northern coast there, for instance, there is no word for "left" or "right"; instead all orientation is done according to compass points, so that you might tell someone, "Your southeast shoe is untied." What's more, in the Thaayorre language, the way to say "hello" translates as "Which way are you going?" and the proper response is along the lines of "West-northwest, in the middle distance," so that if you don't know which way you're pointed, you can't even get past hello.[3]

---

[2] Ascher, Marcia, (1991): *Ethnomathematics*, pp. 132–140. Boca Raton, Fla.: CRC Press.
[3] Boroditsky, Lera. "How Does Our Language Shape the Way We Think?" *Edge* magazine,

Elsewhere on the continent, an account exists[4] from someone who rode with with a small group of Aboriginal people on their first trip in a motor vehicle. They were very quiet before they got underway, but as soon as the Jeep began moving, one of them began telling stories one after another, as fast as he could possibly talk. The stories, it transpired, were traveling stories, meant to be told along this route, which was of course usually traveled at walking pace.

Even in Aussie gift shops run by English-speaking Euro-Australian entrepreneurs, you can find snarky world maps oriented with south at the top of the sheet. (DOWN UNDER NO LONGER, they say.)

But let's take a look at the Western Apache of Arizona, who hold their maps substantially inside their heads rather than on paper. In fact an earnest cartographer would probably find it impossible, even with snazzy gimmicks like Google Earth, to get these maps down satisfactorily: because they extend not only spatially but also temporally and mythologically. Central to the Western Apache's understanding of their world are placenames, which (in compact phrases that become unwieldy in English) carry meanings like "Trail to Life Goes Up" ('Ihi'na' Ha'itin), "Whiteness Spreads Out Descending to Water" (Túzhį' Yaahigaiye'), and "She Carries Her Brother on Her Back" (Kolah Dahch'ewołé). The names attach to even small landscape features like a rock in an evanescent stream, called "Children's Footprints" (Chagháshé Biké'é). These names anchor the place to a story, historical or mythical or somewhere between the two. Moreover, unlike a name such as "New York," which we pass over without any thought as to what a york is or why we needed a new one, or "Oxford," which brings to mind oxen fording a river only for the most peculiarly minded of us, the Western Apache placenames retain enough meaning and emotional power that, after thinking of one, an elder stopped to shake his head and ask, "What were they *thinking*?"[5]

But perhaps the rest of us aren't so different from the Western Apache in that. Much of how we understand our place in the world, we carry around in our heads. Imagine the neighborhood where you grew up. What's on your mental map of it? For me there are suburban houses and busy streets, but in my mind these mostly recede into a desaturated background behind the vividness of the little creeks and woods that I explored with my little brother in those days. A major landmark was the Ivory Tower, a 50-foot-tall white pine that had good climbing branches almost to the very top. From it we could survey everything around us for what seemed to be forever, in our world scaled to that little parcel of half-abandoned parkland in Cincinnati. The importance of that tree and the stories that clustered around it, or around Congress Run and Mill Creek and

---

June 11, 2009. <bit.ly/39hUQZS>

[4]I read this story years ago and can no longer locate the source to name the location or tribe. If it sounds familiar to any reader, I would welcome a note on it.

[5]Basso, Keith (1996): *Wisdom Sits in Places*, pp. 23–29. Albuquerque: Univ. of N.M. Press.

all the places we found along them, aren't transferable to another person, but they're part of a thought-world that he and I share. In their way, those things are little building blocks of a way of life. And all of us see the world through story-maps woven around the material circumstances of our lives.

As those circumstances change, our story-maps will need to, too, if we want to stay afloat. Through learning new tricks as individuals, on to the accumulating differences between generations, the minds of the people of the future will in time be as foreign to us as we find the old Inuit, the Western Apache, or even the wig-powdering denizens of the 1700s Euro-American diaspora, who by and large believed the Earth to be a few thousand years old and slaveholding to be morally defensible.

What will those new maps look like? Well, of course, we can never chart the future in all its detail. But by looking forward with a little wisdom, a little intelligence, and a dose of imagination, we can get somewhere helpfully close. After all, those are exactly the tools that the people who create the future will have at their disposal. And in fact, in writing stories that map out where we may be going, we help *create* that same future we're trying to discover. Because, as we can see when we eye the direct through-line from H. G. Wells to George Lucas and Gene Roddenberry to their result in Elon Musk's spacecapades, the stories we tell are the same ones that those who come after us will use to guide them.

Will the stories in this magazine go on to shape the maps of the future the way those ones did? We can't know that either. But for everyone who reads this, they'll help in at least some small way to fill in the spaces where there be dragons. And anyhow, it's so much fun to just go explore. There's so much territory out there to discover.

Book Reviews

The first time I encountered *Always Coming Home*—sitting on the table of someone I was visiting in northern California, not far from where its stories take place—I opened semirandomly and found a transcription of characters from the village of Chumo having a poetry battle with characters from further down the Valley.

Always Coming Home
Ursula K. Le Guin

> Down the Valley the intelligence of the
>   inhabitants
> is manifested in their custom of brewing
> small beer from dog turds.

> People keep a lot of chickens up in Chumo.
> The chickens are so clever, they talk like people:
> Rock, rock, rock, rock, rock, rock, rockbasket!
> The people in Chumo are as clever as the chickens.

On the next page is a "poem said with the drum" attributed to a character from a different Valley town:

> The hawk turns crying, gyring.
> There is a tick stuck in my scalp.
> If I soar with the hawk,
> I have to suck with the tick.
> O hills of my Valley, you are too complicated!

I didn't quite know what I was looking at, but I knew at least that it wasn't like other books I had read. With a little more paging through, I was satisfied that whatever it was, I would someday need to read the whole thing.

Having finally gotten a copy of my own several years later, I can confirm that it isn't like other books. *Always Coming Home* is not a single story but a collection of texts that weave together to elucidate the complex and quite unfamiliar culture of the Kesh, a people who "might be going to have lived a long, long time from now in Northern California." The culture that you or I would find if we visited the environs of the Napa Valley today is remembered only in stray fragments of folklore, as "the Red Brick People" after the only modern product still remaining after five or ten thousand years, or "the City of Man," which one character visits in a perilous vision to find all the people have their heads on backwards on their shoulders. The shortest of these texts are poems a couple lines long, and the longest the 99 pages of the harrowing life story of an old woman named Stone Telling. They include short plays, songs, a chapter of a novel, personal accounts, pen-and-ink sketches, proverbs, and types of art that we have no word for, like the *tabetupah* or "hearthplay." In the beginning Le Guin asks the reader's forbearance to "bear with some unfamiliar terms [until it] will all be made clear at last," and as you take in more and more, it does come clear in a most satisfying way. You end up with a quite vivid understanding of what the Kesh are like, what they consider wise and unwise, how they understand the world, so that eventually you look at things happening in your own world and think, for example, "Oh, the Kesh would never allow *that* to happen."

If it sounds like there's a pronounced anthropological bent to all this, that's no accident. Le Guin was the daughter of the famous Kroebers (that's what the K. stands for), superstars among ethnographers, to the extent that such phenomena exist. Her mother Theodora wrote the famous *Ishi in Two Worlds*; her father Alfred founded the anthropology department at UC–Berkeley, and was allegedly such an influence to the nascent discipline that a whole generation of young men in that field across the country grew beards just like his. It's interesting to imagine what their dinner table was like; it's known that some of the time it was shared with a Tohono O'odham man, Juan Dolores, who stayed with the family for weeks at a time, teaching the Kroebers about his culture and spending time with them, and in time became like an uncle to young Ursula.

Professorial as this may make the book sound, I believe Le Guin's background should be cause not for suspicion that a dry lecture awaits (it doesn't), but for relief. Having genuinely tried to understand, as much as an outsider may, some cultures vastly different from her own, Le Guin for the most part avoids the common mistake of assuming all cultures are more or less like the mainstream globalized industrial one. So instead of aliens suspiciously like twentieth-century Americans down to the ranks in their military hierarchy (paging General Grievous), here you find Californians so unlike the people alive today that we must concede they live in a different world.

Nor is this, as one reviewer fondly called it, a simple novelization of her parents' studies of the Yurok and Yahi. On a superficial level, it's hard not to note that the Kesh have a little electricity, a powered cotton loom, and even access to something vaguely like the internet, among other modest nifties preserved from the past. But seen more deeply, although her parents' ethnography is clearly present, the Kesh give the impression not of being just like the "first-comers," nor of being pristine Rousseauian nature-people, but of living with wisdom inherited from survivors of a bad period of history, even though that history happened so long ago they know nothing of its stories.

Is it naively utopian? On one hand, of course it is. The Kesh are peaceful, well fed, wine-brewing, sexually liberated, matriarchal wish-fulfillers. Le Guin herself was aware of this problem; a little past the halfway point of the book, she orchestrates a dialogue between herself-as-narrator and a Kesh village archivist, in which she accuses the archivist's world of being a utopia, and the archivist rejoins that it's no such thing—it's "a mere dream dreamed in a bad time ... by a middle-aged housewife, ... a critique of civilization possible only to the civilized, an affirmation pretending to be a rejection, a piece of pacifist jeanjacquerie."

On the other hand, Le Guin's own objections notwithstanding, if it's utopian, we can't accuse it of being naively so. The Valley is not a simple paradise. It has people who are unhappy, for instance, some of them severely so. One charge leveled against the idea that a pacifist culture can exist is that without violent defense capabilities, the people will be easily conquered. The book's longest story serves at least partially as a rebuttal to that charge. It's acknowledged that the Kesh's matriarchy gives men short shrift, risks seeing them as better suited to stay in the gardens and the workshops than to try to grasp the lore of the temples. Not all is well in the Valley, and for that reason we can take these people seriously—their hardships aren't ours, but they're as real as those of fictional people can be, and they don't have easy answers for everything. I respect that. Le Guin stress-tests her utopia for us, and though as its loving creator she may have pulled some punches, still it holds believably firm.

Always Coming Home must stand as a landmark of deindustrial literature, from years before the genre was ever named. Its scope of imagination is vast, encompassing dozens of characters communicating in dozens of kinds of texts; its detail and richness are totally immersive; the possibilities it explores were in large part uncharted before it and many otherwise remain so 35 years later. It is also one of Le Guin's most sympathetic and vulnerable works; readers expecting the austerity of style that marks her other work like *The Dispossessed* and the Earthsea Cycle will find that style colored in with winks, personality, and humor. It is a work of enough complexity that its title page lists not only Le Guin as author but also a composer (an accompanying CD is available), an artist, and a geomancer, though with Le Guin standing at the head as conductor of this symphony.

Always Coming Home was first published in 1985 and has, as far as I can tell, not been reprinted since 2001. Even at the rock-bottom prices of your friendly neighborhood internet megacorporation, a used copy is usually hard to come by for less than $15 US. It's hard to explain the unwarranted obscurity of a work of such breadth by such a famous author. It may be that its unusual structure puts off readers who expected to dive right in at page 1 and read a single narrative straight through to page 525. Or it may be that literature that prophesies a real and final death to our own time and (heresy!) the existence of hope and happiness after it has always had a harder time finding a toehold than space operas and evil AIs. Whatever the case, this is a rewarding book that deserves a place in the deindustrial canon. It will transport you, and may even change your ideas of what a book can do and be.

—*Nathanael Bonnell*

☉

New Maps *welcomes book reviews from readers on deindustrial and related books, fiction and nonfiction, contemporary and past. Essays on deindustrial fiction and the deindustrial future are also considered for publication. To inquire about writing one of these for* New Maps, *please get in touch with the editor at the email or postal address shown on the copyright page.*

STORIES

Pierre Magdelaine

Rhyme and Reason

I

MERYEM GRABBED THE crumpled paper bag and rose from her knees. The man's eyes had closed and the soft afternoon light washed the pain from his face; he appeared to be sleeping. A strong wind blew from the south and disturbed the cloud of flies above his body. Across the railroad tracks, an ash tree shook under the gale.

Meryem stuffed the paper bag in her backpack and walked across the embankment. Dark clouds were gathering in the south and the wind buffeted the plain with sudden blasts. Far to the east, she could just make out the curved line of a road and the orthogonal shape of unidentifiable ruins. The ash tree bent and groaned. Meryem zipped up her rain jacket and wiped the tears from her eyes, walked down the embankment, and set resolutely across the darkening flats.

The storm had flooded the plain. Sparkling rivulets of rainwater trickled from the trees and rushed to constellations of shiny puddles and pools. From afar, the slanting morning light seemed to cover the water in a clear silvery lacquer, but when approached the pools were swallowed by the darkness of the earth, one after the other. The road often disappeared into murky water and Meryem was forced to trudge through rain-soaked fallows, where a thick mud tugged at her boots as if to swallow her. After a few hours, her legs already heavy from exertion, she sat on a tree trunk fallen across the road. She dropped her bag and fished out her bottle. She shut her eyes for a bit. The night had been rough: she'd weathered the storm in a ruined gas station, her tent pitched inside the remaining walls for protection against the wind. After a while, she heaved her pack back on her shoulders and resumed across the flooded plain. The wind had abated after the storm, leaving behind it an eerie quiet in which the squelches of her boots echoed like thunder. Nothing else moved on the brown, deserted country, and neither insects nor birds disturbed its disquieting stillness—

A sudden bark rang out and startled her; she raised her walking stick and turned to see a large dog jump up from behind the rusted carcass of an old pickup truck, bark again and run at her.

"Stop!" she cracked.

The dog froze and lowered its tail. Meryem carefully approached the old, mud-splattered mutt, who must have been at least her own weight and looked tall enough to put his front legs on her shoulders. She knelt down to pat him, and laughed: the dog, sensing the danger had passed, had gone directly for her backpack and was now sniffing at it with great interest.

"Hungry, are we?"

She rose and swung her pack around to take out a slice of jerky.

II

It took them two more days to get to the farm. Meryem's long strides seemed unable to eat away at this dreary expanse of gray grassland stretching endlessly under empty skies. Once in a while, mountains appeared in the distance; their purple silhouettes lit up like will-o'-the-wisps, tugging at Meryem's hopes, before vanishing back into the haze. She was getting wearier by the hour; her thoughts harried her and wheeled around her mind like a buzzing cloud of gnats. The dusty-white sky weighed over her, and the dispiriting silence, underlined by the dog's monotonous panting, gnawed at her heavy heart.

Near the end of the afternoon, Sponger suddenly rushed atop a levee with a happy bark. Shaking with fatigue and anticipation, her mouth dry and her hands sticky with sweat, Meryem climbed after him against a whistling, bitter wind that flattened the yellow grass. On the other side of the levee was the farm, surrounded by rows of fruit trees, its sheet metal roof shining in the sunlight. The dog was making a beeline for a small brick house, toward the smell of roasted meats; Meryem herself stopped for a minute, momentarily lost in a daydream filled with simple pleasures—a warm meal, a shower, a night in the dry.

As soon as she started down, however, her throat tightened. She nervously ran her fingers through her graying hair and licked her cracked lips. The hope she'd contained during her journey was pushing against the levee again. She forced herself to remember she was on a fool's errand, and mined the clutter of past deceptions strewn across her memory to build them up against the bright flood and fortify her heart.

"Hello, ma'am. This your dog?"

A lanky teenage girl was walking up to meet her, dressed in tattered jeans and a faded tank top. She had the tanned skin of one living off the earth.

"Sponger? He's his own dog," Meryem answered.

She tried to smile, but her nerves failed her and twisted her lips into a nervous grin. The girl had frozen halfway up the levee to stare at the yellow cloth tied around her arm. After a moment, her eyes crawled up to Meryem's, who asked:

"Where are the bugs?"

"I wasn't sure you were coming," the farmer said. The afternoon light filtered through the dusty windows and sparkled on the copper and steel pots hung on the walls. "I caught one just this morning. Make yourself comfortable, I'll be just a moment."

Meryem put down her pack and sat at the kitchen table while the man walked away.

"Want a glass of water?" the girl offered.

"Sure."

Meryem realized she was drumming her fingers on the table; she stuck her left hand between her thighs and, with the other, took the glass of water.

"Thanks."

The girl smiled and turned to pet the dog, who was having a go at the remains of a chicken. Meryem put down her glass. Each second the kitchen clock ticked hit the defenses of her rattled soul like a tidal wave. In a last, desperate effort, she reminded herself again that the great black wasps were gone: they had disappeared close to ten years ago, and there was no chance that this farmer had just happened upon a nest. But she also remembered that species had been prematurely declared extinct before and, just like that, hope leaked through the cracks: the black wasps were excellent pollinators, adapted to a wide variety of climates …

"What's it like, being a bug lady?" the girl asked.

"I'm not … it's *entomologist*. Not bug lady."

The girl shrugged and sat opposite her. Her detachment was just as fake as Meryem's: for a girl like her, destined to spend her whole life on the farm where she was born, a yellow armband meant freedom and adventure. Meryem considered her bright eyes and her vigorous, lithe limbs—she was still young, with all of her life before her, while Meryem's was buried in the rubble of her world.

"And because I specialize in wasps, I'm a vespologist."

"Shouldn't it be *wasp*ologist?"

"I don't make up the words, kid."

"So what's it—"

Meryem waved her quiet. The man had come back into room with a mason jar, which he set down on the kitchen table.

"There it is," he said, stepping back and dangling his arms uncomfortably.

Meryem watched the black insect buzz and bump angrily against the walls of its glass prison. When it finally landed on the bottom of the jar and its long thin transparent wings came to lie against the sides of its jet-black body, she was able to examine more closely its oblong abdomen covered with tiny yellowish hair, its sharp mandibles and its delicately elbowed antennae ...

"This isn't a wasp."

The girl was still staring at Meryem with her big green eyes.

"Not a wasp?" her father exclaimed.

Twelve days ... twelve days of hiking across the deserted countryside, trudging through the mud and dust; twelve days of eating seeds, jerky and grits and sleeping under the tent; twelve days of carrying her doubts and her hopes, braving storms and a sweltering sun—all for nothing. The tide she'd striven to contain had infiltrated her defenses and it was now threatening to drown her; she could taste its bitterness on her lips: for all her efforts, some part of her had dared—needed, perhaps—to hope.

"This is an ant," she said hoarsely.

"An ant? But it's got wings!"

"Yeah. It's a male."

She walked out on the front porch and leaned on the railing. The sky was turning a darker shade of blue over the dusty haze. Before her, tidy rows of peach and pear trees stretched their crooked shadows under the evening sun. A dozen or so farmhands were still scattered across the orchard, up on ladders, brushes in hand, leaning over flowers as if to paint them with painstaking care, most of them probably too young to remember a time when hand pollination was yet unnecessary.

Sponger had finished his meal and trotted to her side with a happy bark. He was an optimistic dog—these days, you had to be a dog to be optimistic. Meryem scratched him distractedly behind the ears.

"No more honey," she sang sourly, "means no flavor

> And no flowers means no color
> With the birds their songs have gone
> Give me a reason to carry on
> My love
> In this bland world

This drab world
This silent and dreary world."

III

Meryem spent a troubled night. The barn where the farmer had put her up was much more comfortable than her tent, the straw was dry, she'd showered and her stomach was full, but her thoughts kept whirring with a sick obsession over her memory of the dying man. She heard the flies buzz hungrily about his body, she saw his head lying on the ballast, she saw his sunken, glassy eyes, and she tossed and turned in the dark, haunted by his feverish litany of explanations and supplications. She hadn't known what to say. Would it have mattered? He'd been too far gone to hear her ...

The wind hammered at the barn walls. Sponger let out a grunt and jerked his tail. The crumpled paper bag stood close in the darkness, looking like a strangely shaped idol.

Dawn was yet a paleness over the horizon, and the dark fruit trees still swathed in shadow. The farmhands marched across the orchard with their stepladders under their arms, their heads low and still heavy with sleep. A light breeze made ripples on the pond.

"You're going *east*?" the farmer asked.

"There's someone I have to visit."

Leaning on the railing, Meryem was looking uncertainly eastward, where a pink light was slowly bleeding into the clouds over the horizon.

"Well, you gotta do what you gotta do. I should warn you, though: coast-wards is not safe country, not even for a yellow band."

Meryem didn't know if she liked being called a yellow band any better than a bug lady: it reminded her she belonged to an obsolete guild, which owed its survival solely to the respect its strange rituals commanded among the uninitiated.

"I'm sorry I made you come all this way," the farmer went on. "I really thought ..." He shook his head. "I thought you'd go back home."

She picked up her pack and went her way, and the dog followed.

"It's an eagle," the smallest one said.

"Nah! That's a parakeet!"

Meryem was sitting on the roadside, chewing on a loaf of bread. The kids had barreled out of the cornfield like cannon balls and run past her without a glance before stopping dead under a power line, transfixed by the sight of the big black bird perched on the wire.

"Ain't no parakeet, you bonehead," the third one said. "And it ain't no eagle neither."

"Oh yeah? Well then what is it?"

The kid smiled broadly.

"It's a pigeon!"

The three of them burst into laughter, causing the raven to caw and jerk its head in their direction. The kids shut up and froze, petrified by the bird's kingly stare. Meryem wiped her hands with a thin smile. She stood and walked resignedly back on the dilapidated road. Upon leaving the farm, she had long ruminated over her decision to set out on a dangerous journey toward the coast, straight into a storm-ravaged land, just so she could try—and most likely fail—to accomplish a stranger's dying wish. All day the memory of the dying man had stirred in his mind—the rusty rail against his head, the heavy blue sky, the creaking ash tree ... and his tangled and confused words, which he'd repeated over and over, like a chorus: "Tell her I love her ... tell her she must forget me, and love another ..." The wind had picked up. Flies had lighted on his mouth; she'd waved them away with a burst of indignation. The smell ... it would never leave her.

At sundown she had pitched her tent in a fallow field. She'd fallen asleep instantly, exhausted by her hike and the constant attacks of her doubts; by the next morning, she'd come to the conclusion that it made just as much sense to go on as to go back home.

Evening's purple shadows bled over the flats, blurring the line between earth and sky and turning the clouds into distant mountains. Two silhouettes had appeared by an old car wreck stranded on the grassy roadside. Sponger barked, and a third shadow rose from the car.

Meryem paused. She looked over her shoulder: another shadow had come out of the brush behind her. She walked on. The silhouettes were getting more distinct as she got closer; soon she realized that what she'd mistaken for broad chests and shoulders were only tatters and rags much too large for the scraggy youngsters who wore them.

"Got any food in that backpack, ma'am?" came a raspy voice.

"Not much."

They weren't teenagers anymore, but not yet adults either—kids still, with long faces and empty stomachs. Their long shadows stretched across the road and spilled into the brush. Meryem had stopped. Steps were coming up behind her.

"Care to share?" offered one of them, flicking open a switchblade. Sponger growled. Meryem tightened her grip on her walking stick.

"As I said, it isn't much."

She turned so that they could not miss her yellow arm band. The kid with the knife paused.

"Whatcha waiting for?" snarled another, his long crowbar glinting menacingly.

Meryem stepped aside and noticed the silhouette coming up behind her had stopped a dozen paces from her. The kid with the knife couldn't bring himself to take a decision, and the others seemed to be waiting for him. Meryem took another step back. Sponger growled threateningly, his hackles raised.

The one with the crowbar pushed the other aside and walked decidedly toward her; Sponger barked and Meryem steeled herself—

"Stop."

The last shadow had grabbed her companion by the shoulder. He turned to her angrily.

"This isn't worth it. You want people to hear we done a yellow band?"

The crowbar kid threw Meryem and her armband a scathing look, and stepped aside to let her pass.

Every day they were getting closer to the coast. There was no dramatic change of scenery—the empty roads still cut across fallow fields scattered with wild thickets, farms where the land had been spared by the storms, and pools of stagnant water—but the farms were getting scarcer, and the pools bigger. One day, they passed a field that was completely swamped. A few ears of grain poked up from the still waters, beneath squadrons of gnats and flies whose incessant buzzing sounded like a rattle. Meryem looked up toward the southeast, where it was said there was more water than land now, and she was overwhelmed once more by the absurdity of her quest. She remembered the dry smell of the ballast and that of the moribund; she remembered the rocks cutting into her knees as she knelt on the ballast—and yet back then she had not been conscious of the pain, only of the sorrow and regret in the man's eyes, and of the mad hope that had flourished in his smile as he'd said: "Tell her I love her ... tell my son I wished I'd known him and I'm proud of him ...."—everything else just background noise.

Sponger rubbed his head against her leg. The brown silhouette of a lark flew past and landed on the road to peck at an ear of grain. Meryem affectionately scratched Sponger's neck and squashed a gnat on her arm. "I've paid for what I've done, ma'am," the man had explained, his voice between a whisper and a wheeze, "ten long years. And she's waited, you know, she's waited. And my son—she wrote me about him ... Tell her I love her. Tell her she must forget me, and love another." She'd found herself nodding and wiping tears away from her face. She'd taken the paper bag, and the dying man had muttered something that sounded like a blessing.

Meryem started again, her pack and her doubts weighing equally heavy on her back. Ten years in jail ... how changed the world must have looked to him! She tried to remember what her life had been like ten years ago—it was another woman's life. And those were the words guiding her? The words of a man from another time, of a dying and delirious man? She wasn't any more likely to find his wife than she was those wasps. All she had to go on was the woman's name, and the fact that she lived on the coast ... few people still lived there, but there was a reason for that. How many hurricanes had hit in the last ten years? This woman had probably gone away after the third or the fourth, like everyone else ... if she had the chance.

IV

Two days later they came upon a small town with only a few houses left, perched on stilts and huddled around a church. The evening light fell in long shadows over the muddy streets, and the whitewashed steeple leaned slightly northwards, like an arrow stuck in the sky's side. Before the church was a billboard with the service hours and a scripture quote: THEY HAVE SOWN THE WIND; THEY SHALL REAP THE WHIRLWIND. HOSEA 8:7. A crow sat atop the sign, eyeing Meryem quizzically.

"Evening, ma'am," a man greeted her from his front porch, where he was reclining with a wide-brimmed hat lowered over his brow. He had the local drawl, and his wicker chair rocked with a melancholic creak. Meryem felt her heart and throat constrict. Wherever she went—even here, to the far reaches of the earth—she couldn't let go of her nostalgia. Like everyone, she was obsessed about the past—after all, most of the insect species she'd learned about when she was a student were extinct now ... it was like knowing a dead language, and the prestige it gave her resembled that of the scholars who'd kept speaking in Latin after the Roman Empire had collapsed.

"Evening, sir," she answered. "I'm looking for someone. Maybe you could help me?"

But of course he didn't know the girl.

"You should try the church," he counseled. "Many people pass through here on their way north and most stop by the church. Our minister, he's good with names and faces."

☉

The minister had heard of a family who'd decided to stay, way down south on the coast; a single mother with her son.

"She has a name like Daisy, or Lily …"

"Or Rose?"

"Could be."

"Come on, Sponger. Let that bone be, we're going south."

The further south they went, the more water surrounded them. Pools and ponds became lakes, and finally swamps. Once in a while they would come upon the ruins of a forsaken farm. In some places, storms had caused the road's embankment to collapse, and Meryem had to trudge through the mire and run the risk of losing her boots.

One night, she thought she might never find ground dry enough to pitch her tent; after the sun had set and twilight had faded to a purple shadow on the horizon, she finally resolved to sleep on the pavement. The next morning, all land had disappeared: the new day was rising over a vast expanse of rippling amber—only the straight line of the road, thickets of reeds, and lines of trees remained, emerging from the waters like the remains of a pastoral Atlantis. Meryem packed up her tent and set off with Sponger. Water and sky had awoken with them: gnats and flies flitted around them in a low buzz, bright dragonflies darted blue and green in the salty air, ducks and thrushes cried and trilled in the rushes—songs on the wind, and colors over the waters. Sponger trotted happily before Meryem, mesmerized by this exuberant display of life, racing after a duck and running back to her yapping happily.

Toward the end of the morning, Sponger barked and rushed forward, causing a flock of terns to scatter in fright. Meryem took a long whiff. At first, she could only smell the dank, salty swamp water lapping sleepily on both sides of the embankment, but then the wind turned and she caught it: smoke, frying fish. The perspective of a warm meal emerged in her mired mind. Her stomach rumbled. She followed the curve of the road around a flooded thicket of trees, toward a thin column of smoke, and on the right-hand side of the road she spotted a boy, about ten years old, standing in shallow waters. She stopped. The boy waved to her, turned, and leaned back into the water.

"I'm Rose," the woman answered, kneeling by the dog and patting him. The old freeloader was already halfway through an eel. "Why do you ask?"

Meryem didn't answer. She looked out the window at the waste of water, shimmering with wind and sunlight.

"And the boy, outside …"

"That's my son Paul. We've been by ourselves for a long time, but his father will be back soon." She must have read something on Meryem's face, because her smile turned into a perplexed frown. "Why don't you sit down?" she offered. "You must be tired."

"Thank you."

Meryem sat and rummaged through her backpack. She took out the crumpled paper bag and put it on the table.

"He was on his way here …" she started.

Sponger had finished and was looking up at her silently. Rose was still by his side, patting him, as if to avoid opening the paper bag, but she couldn't take her eyes off it. Meryem cleared her throat.

"He asked me to tell you he loved you," she went on. "He said you should forget him, and love someone else … he asked me …" She met Rose's glistening eyes. "He asked me to tell his son he wished he'd met him."

Rose wiped her eyes. Sponger put his head on her knees; she rubbed him and scratched his neck with a grateful smile.

"Do you like eels, Meryem?"

The rich smell of frying fish filled the little house; birdsongs wafted in through the open window; freshly cut swamp flowers floated in a bowl on the kitchen table—flavor, music, and color; rhyme and reason.

Dawn Vogel

Hearts in Motion

My PARENTS WOULD have killed me if they knew I was speeding downhill in the old shopping cart. Since I'd have to haul it back to the village later, full of whatever I'd scavenged, I wanted to save myself some work early in the day. Anyway, I had my trusty steering stick, which kept me from running into hazards.

At least it should have.

Jamming my steering stick into a rock outcropping, in an outwash I'd navigated a hundred times before, my stick stuck in the rocks, my hands slipped from the grip, and I was careening down the hill at top speed without my stick.

My heart raced. If I leaned to either side of the shopping cart, I could correct my course some, but if I leaned too far, I'd topple the whole thing, leaving me banged up, if not broken and dead.

I was headed straight for the old pool complex. A wide swath of cracked concrete and scrubby foliage, inhabited by scorpions, snakes, and other desert critters, in the shadow of the diving platform, it was filled with perils to the casual visitor on foot, let alone someone flying into it at top speed.

Amongst the spindly cacti that had clawed their way up between the cracks, someone moved. It had to be a human—they were too big and too upright to be one of the many animals that made their home there. They dragged something long, narrow, and white across the shallow end of the pool. It stretched across the entire pool, evenly spaced white mesh squares, surprisingly intact for something in the desert.

A net? It had to be a trap, set to stop unwary scavengers like me.

If I tipped the shopping cart here, the rocky terrain would dash my brains out, the spindly plants shredding my skin to ribbons. My only chance was to roll right into the trap and hope that I could slice through the net with my utility knife. I tucked myself into a ball and braced for impact, my heartbeat pounding

25

in my ears.

The net strained when the cart hit, slowing my momentum. Everything paused, and then the cart shot backward. The slope rolled it back into the net, then bounced it off a few more times. I was rattled, but not trapped.

As the shopping cart stopped, I stood, ready to defend myself or run, as circumstances required. I scanned the area for the person who had set this trap.

A girl about my age—sixteen or so—stood at one end of the net, her head tilted to the side, a smile playing across her lips. "Are you alright?" she asked.

She was tall, slender, and pale, shrouded in flowing fabrics that covered her skin and most of her hair, except for one straight lock that was whiter than the painted concrete of the pool.

I was speechless. I'd just narrowly escaped death, but the words vanished because of her. She'd saved me. My cynical side wondered why, but my heart didn't care.

"What—why—" I shook my head to clear it and put away my knife, certain the threat of a trap was no more. "Uh, yes, I'm alright."

"Good. It's dangerous to ride a shopping cart around here."

"Yeah, my parents keep telling me. I'm Ayo."

"Everly."

I scanned the diving platform, the pool beneath. "You live here?"

She shrugged. "Near here. You?"

I gestured back over my shoulder. "The village."

"Oh." Her tone spoke volumes. Village folk didn't associate with desert folk, and vice versa. "I should go."

"Me too."

"Okay." Everly returned to the end of the net and began untying it from the post.

I climbed from my shopping cart, no longer willing to risk riding. I glanced back at Everly as I walked, always jerking my gaze away when I found she was watching me too, both of us blushing when our eyes met.

I snuck out of the village late that night, without my shopping cart. The full moon illuminated the white diving platform, a beacon in the desert wasteland. Even if it hadn't been so bright, I couldn't have missed the slight figure on the second platform, leaning against the central tower, facing the village. My heart sang.

The ladder was well maintained, some of the repairs visible. Someone had taken good care of this place. I climbed to where Everly sat. She'd seen me coming. I hadn't tried to sneak.

"Ayo. Hi."

"Hi." My tongue felt too big for my mouth, my throat full of sand, my heart pounding. All the questions I wanted to ask slipped from my mind.

"Do you want to sit?"

I nodded, took a seat beside her, but gave her some space.

She scooted toward me, then paused, eyes wide but uncertain.

I scooted closer too.

Neither of us knew a thing about the other, but here we were.

"Thank you for saving me," I whispered.

She chuckled. "Thank you for not attacking me on sight."

"Why would I—?"

"Why wouldn't you? Desert folk." She pointed at herself.

"But you saved me. Who cares?"

"My parents. Your parents. Everyone else in the world?"

I reached my arms out tentatively.

Everly scooted closer to me, letting me wrap my arms around her. She rested her head on my chest, just above my heart. "Tell me about the village."

"Only if you tell me about the desert next."

Daniel Chawner

The Inspector's Legacy

AT FIRST LIGHT, the *Muni 14* glided into Raritan Bay. She had anchored offshore until the Verrazano signal fires indicated the all-clear. Thin black smoke wafted from the cargo vessel's main stack as it passed the Hook sandbar and motored into a narrow corridor of buoys. The hulking remains of three rusted destroyers appeared to its port in the gray November morning, clustered around a long, narrow naval pier. Smaller wooden fishing boats in various stages of decay dotted the calm, flat water off the starboard side.

Two spotters in sun-bleached blue coveralls stood on the bow. As they passed Old Naval Station Earle, they could see the blinking red lights of two Muni Zodiacs ahead on either side of the channel.

A low whistle rose from the destroyer closest to the *Muni 14*, barely audible over the clank of the cargo ship's diesel engine. The spotters watched as a wiry man with a thick gray beard, shaved head, and loose green pants threw a grease-stained burlap sack onto the cargo ship's deck. A deckhand in blue picked it up and headed into the bridge. The captain stuck his head out the window and waved to the bearded man, who saluted and disappeared into the destroyer.

"Should we open it?" asked the deckhand.

After a lengthy pause, the captain exhaled and nodded his head.

The deckhand kneeled and poured out the contents of the sack. Several green nails, spikes, and copper coins clattered across the floor. A large waxy leaf, folded and sewn shut with rough twine, appeared amongst the salvage.

"Message," said the captain, holding out his hand.

The deckhand handed the leaf to the captain. "What does it say?"

"Never you mind. Back to your post. Take the gifts and give them to the crew."

The deckhand collected the metal salvage into the sack. When the heavy door of the bridge slammed shut again, the captain turned his attention to the bay and ignored the nervous churn in his stomach.

Peter waddled into the crowded cafeteria on the second floor of the Muni Health Department tower. He passed a long line of workers in red coveralls waiting for their turn at the large breakfast buffet at the front. He headed to a table with two men wearing yellow coveralls like his own.

"Good day, gentleman," said Peter in his high, nasal voice.

The older man scratched his face through his gray beard and grunted back at Peter.

His tablemate, a slender, dark-skinned man, said, "Hello, sir."

Peter set down his clipboard and stepped up to the buffet. As he approached, workers in red stepped out of his way. He grabbed a tray and shoveled hard-boiled eggs, tomatoes, blueberries, and kelp cakes onto two plates.

From somewhere at the back of the line, a worker shouted, "Rationing, please!"

A chorus of hushes ensued.

Peter scowled over his shoulder, then took his laden tray back to his table and sat heavily on the bench. The younger man at the table gasped at the piles of food on his plates.

"Our fine chickens look to be back in good health." Peter sliced into a hard-boiled egg. "It's been weeks. I've missed them so."

He looked up, a fork full of egg poised in front of his mouth. "How is everyone today? Richard, how are you feeling?"

"Fine, Peter, just fine," the older man said. He nodded toward the man seated across from him. "Peter, this is Srinivas. He will train with us for the next few months."

Peter extended his hand. "Peter Arbuckle the Third."

Sri shook his hand. "Yes, sir, I know. A pleasure to meet you."

"And are you enjoying the medley of delectable fare from our fine department?"

Sri scrunched his face, looked over at Richard, and shrugged.

"Peter just asked if you like the Health Department food," said Richard.

"Ah, of course. Yes, sir, very much. And I also like that we can take extras home to our family."

"And what is your full name, if I may?" Peter asked before taking a mouthful of egg.

Richard frowned. "Peter, there's no need—"

"No, I don't mind," Sri said. "Srinivas Rao. Originally from New Jersey, south of the Raritan."

"I've known Sri's family for years. They live in the same settlement as my brother."

"Ah, first generation with the department," Peter said. "What does your family do?"

Richard frowned at him again.

"My parents and grandparents worked in the Power Department, on the engineering teams," Sri said. "I got into the Health Department apprenticeship through the lottery."

Peter swallowed his food. "Hmm … and will you move to Fresh Kills Heights with the rest of us?"

"Yes, once my apprenticeship is over and I become a full inspector. *If* I become a full inspector, sir."

"Excellent." Peter attacked the tomatoes and kelp cakes.

"Sri will train with me for these first few weeks," Richard said. "Then I'll have him work with you, especially on the food distro inspections."

Peter nodded. "So why did you want to join the Health Department, Sri? Why not stay as a legacy with Power?"

"Power is boring, static. And it doesn't have the prestige or the perks of the Health Department."

Peter nodded vigorously. "Indeed, indeed."

"What do you have on the agenda for today, Peter?" asked Richard.

"I have to check the log. There could be some dock work, or possibly the East Side satellite kitchen. They had an incident a few days ago."

A teenaged boy in orange coveralls stepped up to the table with a battered manila envelope in hand. "Head Inspector Richard Schmidt the Fourth?"

"Yes, thank you." Richard accepted the envelope.

When the messenger left, Richard unwound the red string on the envelope and pulled out a narrow slip of paper. He studied the slip, looked up with a pause, then looked down at the slip again.

"Everything all right, sir?" asked Peter.

Richard switched his gaze between Sri and Peter. "Change of plan, gents. Peter, I need you to take Sri today. Go to the West Side processing plant, show him how to do a proper top-down inspection."

"But, sir, I just did an inspection there last week! They did quite well, exemplary in fact."

Richard leaned in and spoke slowly, in a voice barely above a whisper. "I need you to take Sri today. On an inspection. I don't care if you just did the processing plant. Do it again."

Peter scrunched up his face. He glanced at Sri, then dropped his eyes. "Yes, sir."

"I'll catch up with you both in the office later today. I have a meeting with the banking liaison in the early afternoon. Sri, pay attention to how Peter does his work. He is the most meticulous inspector Manhattan has ever seen."

Peter smiled widely as Richard pushed up from the table, grabbed his tray, and headed out of the cafeteria. He then turned his attention to his charge. "So, it's just the two of us today? Splendid, splendid. Have you seen any food inspections yet?"

"No, not yet. I've only worked in the Outerborough Administration office until now. This is my first day in Manhattan, ever."

"Well, this will be a treat then. I'll give you the grand tour. Let's get to it, shall we?"

Peter stood up from the table, grabbed his clipboard, and headed toward the door. Sri collected the remaining trays and trotted after him.

The inspectors left the Health Department tower on Madison and 42nd. They walked up the middle of Madison Avenue, past blocks of empty buildings with windows covered in plywood. Large chunks of building facade littered the sidewalks.

When they reached 47th Street, they stopped.

"That way will take us to the West Side plant." Peter pointed west. "But since this is your first day in the field, let's get a better view of things."

Peter ambled eastward, and Sri followed him closely.

"This area is mostly vacant," Peter continued, "except for some Muni workers. These buildings are just homes for the rats at this point. At least until the Banker Line."

"The Banker Line is a real thing? Like a line in the street?" Sri tried to match Peter's dawdling pace but struggled to avoid walking ahead of him.

"It's not official, of course, but it's very real, at least to me. There, at 50th Street, where all the rickshaw drivers are stationed—that's the Banker Line."

Above 50th, the streets were clear of debris. Enforcement workers in orange coveralls stood on street corners. All of the buildings' windows were intact. Rounded glass passageways connected the buildings a few stories above street level.

"Those rickshaws are for the bankers?" Sri asked.

"No, bankers mostly traverse via the skyways between buildings. The rickshaws are mainly for Munis who need to move around during the day and for larger deliveries. Come on, let's go to the wall."

They headed toward the towering seawall that encompassed Manhattan.

"It looks so big from here," Sri said. "It looks smaller from the outside, from the bay."

"Yes, it's more than forty feet above street level. And it goes below street level as well, driven into the layers beneath us. It was originally only twenty-five feet, but they added more two generations ago, after the third flood."

On Lexington Avenue, Peter stopped in front of a low-grade ramp that led to the top of the wall. He squinted into the open door of a garage on the corner.

"Hello, good man. Yes, hello?"

A worker in brown coveralls looked out at them, then quickly turned and walked to the back of the garage, past an assortment of rickshaws, bikes, and sleds.

"Yes, hello," Peter repeated. "You there! I see you. Please, we require assistance."

The man turned and faced him from across the garage. "Yes, Inspector?"

"We need a ride to the top of the wall."

The man's shoulders slumped forward, and he said something under his breath.

Peter put his hands on his hips. "As soon as you can, please." His voice was higher than usual.

The man piloted a cycle rickshaw out of the garage and stopped in front of the two men in yellow. Peter settled into the back seat, and Sri squeezed in beside him. The man turned the rickshaw around and started to head away from the wall.

"No, we need to get to the top of the wall!" Peter shouted.

"Yes," growled the driver, "but we need to build momentum first. I'm not a machine."

They headed about a hundred feet down 47th before the man made a U-turn. He then began to pedal vigorously as he approached the ramp. The wheels of the rickshaw hit the ramp with a thud, and he continued to quickly pump his legs. Standing out of his seat, he steadily cranked the pedals, puffing as he went. Midway up the ramp, the grade flattened out, and the man rested briefly to catch his breath. He stood on the pedals again when the incline continued farther up the wall.

The inspectors hopped off the rickshaw at the top of the ramp.

Peter stepped to the outside parapet of the ten-foot-wide crest atop the wall. "The view here is quite something, yes?"

Sri joined him and took in the view. Below and to the north, a long, wide dock stretched out from the wall. Workers in red and blue emptied cargo from small ships on the north side of the dock. On the south side, closest to the two inspectors, floated a battered cargo ship. MUNI 14 was painted across her bow.

The Queensboro Bridge, with its painted steel trusses, lurked in the distance. The only remaining East River bridge, it carried thick power cables from the Outerborough to Manhattan. Workers in the brown coveralls of the Power

Department dotted the expanse.

Peter turned to speak to the rickshaw driver. "Good man, we—"

But the man had already turned his vehicle around and was rolling down the ramp.

Peter sighed. "We'll have to find another way down."

Sri shrugged absently.

"My father used to take me up here when I was a kid," Peter said. "Showed me how things flowed into the city and how the Health Department was integral to its safety and security. When he got his start, they still had a lot of problems with food waste, food disappearing, shortages in the bankers' dining halls. He helped improve the whole system, solved a lot of those problems."

Sri interrupted Peter. "Is that kelp aboard that cargo ship, Inspector?"

"Ah, yes, that's a ship awaiting inspection, as I suspected. The *Muni 14* is in from the kelp fields. This should be quite instructive."

A figure in yellow walked through the crowd on the dock and headed toward the gangplank.

"Ah, perfect," Peter said. "Here's our Richard. We can watch him run the inspection."

"But, sir," Sri said, "aren't we supposed to do a Chapter 12 Food Inspection, like the Head Inspector told us?"

"We'll get there in good time. Like I said, I just performed an inspection there. Besides, they run the tightest process in Manhattan. There's plenty of time for that and a hearty lunch."

Sri bit his lip.

"This will be enlightening. Don't worry." Peter pointed down to the busy dock area.

On the dock, workers pushed a large crane down a set of tracks next to the cargo ship. Others stood in groups, shouting to the deckhands.

Next to Richard, a short, stocky woman in green coveralls carried a huge bag over her shoulder.

"Notice the bag that techie is carrying?" Peter asked. "Do you know what that is?"

"I think it's the inspection tools," Sri said. "The pad and sensors?"

"Yes, very good." Peter wrinkled his nose. "These loathsome techies are very protective of their tools and machines. They don't trust us to carry or store the tools ourselves. That's really their only job, to keep these gadgets running. Anyway, the techie will wait on the dock. Protocol states they can't take part in the actual inspection."

Richard took the bag from the tech worker and stepped onto the *Muni 14*, where he met two men in blue. The one wearing an old-fashioned captain's hat shook hands with him and handed over a sheaf of papers.

Peter and Sri watched as Richard performed the first few steps of the inspection. Peter provided a running commentary to Sri as the Head Inspector examined the manifest, checked the crew's health, and recorded information from the gauges attached to the kelp beds.

"Ah, here's the probe," Peter said. "This is really the key part of the inspection. Everything else could be okay, but if there's an issue with the kelp itself, he'll have to fail it, of course."

"So the probe detects infected kelp?"

"No! Goodness gracious, man, do they teach you anything in training? The probe can't detect infected kelp. That kind of test requires labs and scientists. Maybe pre-flood, pre-pandemic they could do that for each shipment. The best we can do now is make sure the conditions that contamination causes, in terms of temperature and appearance, aren't there."

Peter pulled a spiced kelp cake from the front pocket of his coveralls and took a large bite.

The inspectors watched Richard climb the bed ladder with the probe attached to a glowing pad. He reached out and placed the probe near the center of the bed. After a slight pause, the pad screen turned bright green, easily visible to the inspectors on top of the wall. Richard then shifted the probe deeper into the bed. Again, the pad glowed green.

Peter swallowed his kelp cake and belched. "Ah, it looks like the bed is clean. He just needs to take a picture of some kelp, save the data, and be on his way."

Richard climbed down from the ladder and pointed to the deck. The captain kneeled and dumped a pile of withered blue kelp from a pouch in his coveralls. Richard then stuck the end of the probe into the pile. The pad glowed bright red. Richard positioned the pad over the kelp and then nodded to the captain. The captain returned the kelp to its pouch and handed it to the other man in blue, who disappeared through the kelp beds.

Sri looked over at Peter, who stared down at the ship. Peter continued watching as Richard put the tools away in the bag, shook hands with the captain, and headed toward the gangplank.

"I don't know what he's doing." Peter said it so softly that Sri could barely hear him.

Upon returning to the dock, Richard said something to the captain. He then removed a red placard from the bag and slapped it on a small pegboard next to the gangplank.

The men on the dock broke out of their respective groups. Most of them headed back toward the wall gate. Some positioned themselves around the crane and pushed it away from the ship. The deckhands began working on the moorings.

"He failed them," Peter said. "He failed the entire shipment. But it was clean."

"What happens to all that kelp now?" Sri asked.

"Well, what's supposed to happen is the ship heads out to one of the dead zones offshore to dump the contaminated cargo. And keeps a manifest." Peter turned to face Sri. "But I don't know what just happened here."

Peter watched the *Muni 14* cast off from the dock. He tapped his clipboard against his beefy thigh. Sri stood next to him, shuffling his feet.

"We have to stop that ship," Peter muttered.

"What's that?"

"We need to speak with the harbormaster. Come, he's further down the wall."

Sri grabbed Peter's arm. "Please! Please, sir. This is my first day as a trainee. The Head Inspector told us to do the food intake inspection, and he'll decide if I become an inspector. I don't want to get in trouble, sir."

Peter looked down at Sri's hand on his arm, then up at Sri with bulging eyes. Sri pulled back his hand.

"What do you know about the department?" Peter asked him. "How we came to enjoy the position we find ourselves in today?"

"What I learned in the Academy. The Manhattan Muni government was formed, and it established the five departments: Health, Power, Enforcement, Shipping, and Technology. They considered the Health Department the front line of defense against the pandemics and the food- and water-borne outbreaks. So they, er, we got a lot of support and authority in the Muni. Then—"

"Yes, yes, yes. That's all true. But you left out the most important part."

Sri was about to say something but stopped. He shrugged instead.

Peter held his clipboard aloft. "We are the protectors of Manhattan. The global bankers and the remains of the United States federal government are all here on this island. They rely on us to make sure the food they eat, the water they drink, and the people they meet won't make them sick. An illness of any type, whether from a bad batch of kelp or another Quick Flu, could bring the entire system down."

Sri nodded.

"So we have our rules, our inspections, our procedures," Peter continued, "but, most of all, we have our ethics. My father, who was Richard's boss and mentor years ago, drove that into me. We must be methodical. We have to, above everything else, do what is right. For Muni, for Manhattan, for the people we serve."

Peter tried to calm himself by taking several deep breaths. He looked down at his clipboard. "We have to report and stop that ship."

He wheeled around and marched toward the harbormaster's office.

The office was a long, narrow pillbox with windows facing the East River. A steel ladder ran down the front of the seawall, just outside a side door. A ramp leading to the street below sloped down from the rear of the building.

Peter knocked on the harbormaster's door. "Hello? Hello! We have urgent business."

Sri rolled his eyes.

The heavy steel door swung open.

A thin, blond-haired man in his twenties wearing the orange coveralls of the Enforcement Department opened the door. "Oh, hey, Inspector. What's up?"

"There's something afoul with that vessel below," Peter said. "We need to arrest its departure."

The man cocked his head to one side.

"He means he wants you to stop that cargo ship from leaving the dock," said Sri. "Please."

The man glanced over his shoulder to the papers spread out under the windows. "We were just signaled they failed inspection. They need to dump their cargo. Now you want us to stop it?"

"Yes." Peter pushed his bulk toward the office door. "Exactly what I said."

The man backed up. "Ah, I can signal them to stop, but it will cause—"

"What do you think you're doing?" shouted a raspy voice from inside the office.

"This inspector from the Health Department is asking to stop that cargo vessel that just failed."

A tall, barrel-chested man stepped toward the door. "Is that you, Arbuckle?"

The blond-haired man faded back into the office.

Peter, who had been leaning against the doorjamb, stood up straight. "Yes, Peter Arbuckle the Third." He backed away from the doorway, retreating from the harbormaster's advance.

The harbormaster had greasy black hair, deep lines in his tanned face, and thick shoulders and arms. He towered over the much shorter and softer Peter.

"Arbuckle, what do you want? Nothin' for you to get involved in up here."

"We need to stop that ship, Luis."

"What? What ship?"

"That one." Peter pointed to the *Muni 14*. It had dropped its mooring lines and pulled away from the dock.

Luis laughed. "Well, before I tell you to pound sand, I gotta know. Why do you think I should stop the *Muni 14*?"

"Because the cargo, the kelp, is clean. It should be processed, not dumped."

"You Health Department boys are quite a trip. They signaled that the kelp failed."

"Yes, that's the dilemma. It failed, but I fear the kelp is fine and needs to be ..."

Luis stepped up to Peter, his chest pressing against the shorter man's clipboard. "Here's your real dilemma. You're standing here, on my wall, telling me what to do with my harbor. Get out of here, Arbuckle the Third. Now."

Peter stood his ground, wide-eyed. He coughed at the powerful tobacco odor from Luis's breath. "If you'd just listen to what we have to say."

"I've heard enough." Luis turned away. "Oh, and say hello to your father for me," he said as he slammed the heavy door behind him.

"Well, that went well," said Sri.

Peter watched the *Muni 14* follow an Enforcement skiff. The two vessels floated to the center of the East River, marked by buoys and the decayed pilings of old bridges.

Out of the other side of the harbormaster's office, the blond-haired Enforcement worker jumped on a cycle rickshaw and rolled down to the street.

Peter pushed open the door to the main entrance of the Health Department Inspectors' office. Red-faced, he stood in the doorway and panted.

A woman glanced up at him from behind a metal desk. "Peter! What's wrong, honey? You look like you ran around Manhattan. Sit down and have some water."

Peter walked over to the desk. Sweat beaded on his forehead. "Jessica, we have a situation. Most urgent."

"I'm sure, Peter, but you need to slow down. You're all worked up! Remember your blood pressure, just like your father's."

"I require your immediate assistance. Please let me know the whereabouts of the Head Inspector."

Jessica leaned back into her green padded chair. She had long blond hair, oversized glasses, and a black dress that clung to her thin frame. Her official red coveralls hung over the back of her chair. "You want to know where Richard is?"

"Yes, have you seen him? I believe he has a meeting with the liaison today."

Jessica moved aside a pile of yellow and grey papers and pulled out a spiral notebook labeled Planner. "Let's see ... Where are we...?" She turned the pages and ran her finger up each one. "Okay, here we are, today. Yes, Richard's meeting with the liaison ..." She leaned to her left and looked around Peter at the clock on the wall. "In twenty minutes." She looked past him again. "And who's this?"

Peter half turned and saw Sri a few feet behind him. "Ah, this is our newest trainee, Srinivas Rao. Perhaps you can show him some procedures for filing reports? He can stay here with you, yes?"

"We'll get our weekly Power Hour during the liaison meeting. Does Srinivas want to learn about entering data and printing?"

Sri looked around the crowded office on the second floor of the Health

Department tower. Piles of papers, banks of file cabinets, and rows of desks filled the space. Two men in green coveralls pushed a cart loaded with silver laptops and dangling power cords to the center of the room.

Peter stormed past Jessica and disappeared into the stairwell. Sri and Jessica locked eyes.

"He wouldn't listen to me," Sri said. "I tried to get him to do the food inspection we were assigned to, but he insisted on racing back here."

Jessica motioned toward the stairwell with her head. Sri nodded and caught up with Peter on the third-floor landing.

Peter pushed open the stairwell door into a large room filled with workers in red and three long tables. They clustered around a table beneath the large east windows. A pile of broken kelp cakes covered a table in the middle of the room. Bursts of laughter and rhythmic drumming on a hollow can met the two inspectors. Peter walked midway through the space and stopped.

One hand on his hip, the other gripping his clipboard, Peter scanned the room. The drumming ceased. The workers lowered their voices and turned toward the two inspectors.

Richard's voice rang out from a smaller room on the far side of the large hall. "Peter! Are you lost?" The men sitting with him snickered.

Peter marched into the Head Inspector's office. He stood there and glared at Richard. "Gents, can I get the room?"

The workers grabbed their coffee mugs and filed out of the Head Inspector's office.

One of the workers, a man with grey-streaked hair and a neat beard, paused before leaving. "Hey, P.A.-Three, good to see you again."

Peter nodded back to him. He'd known Augie since the day his father took him into work as a boy. He was now a senior foreman.

The small office barely held a rectangular table surrounded by five chairs. Peter sat down next to Richard, who claimed the chair at the head of the table. LIAISON MEETING and a grid of numbers were scrawled in white chalk on a chipped blackboard behind Richard. Sri stood near the door.

Richard looked over at Peter and spread his arms. "What is it?"

"Sir, Head Inspector, we saw something today that I need to speak to you about. I wanted to give Sri an overview of our operation before going to the inspection you assigned us to."

"And?"

"So we went to the wall. On the wall—"

"Yes, I know what happened."

Peter cocked his head at him. "You do?"

"You watched me inspect the kelp shipment. Then you went to the harbor-master's office to stop the ship from leaving. Then came back here. That sound about right?"

Peter nodded. Richard looked up at Sri, who also nodded but kept his attention on his feet.

"Sir, I need to know what happened," Peter said. "Why did you fail that shipment?"

Richard rubbed his face with both hands. He then opened and closed his mouth. "I'm not sure where to start."

"How about the part where you falsified your inspection and violated our oath?"

"Okay, let's start there. Yes, I did those things, and I did them knowingly." Richard shifted in his chair. He leaned forward and placed his elbows on the table. "But there are some other things in the world, in my world, that sometimes take precedence. Okay?"

"No," said Peter. "We both learned from my father that the oath we took, the one that gives us our job, our position, our mandate, is the most important thing. He had me learn it when I was a boy."

"Our job here, to keep the bankers and government folks healthy, is important—very important—and I take it seriously, just like all the other inspectors do. What I'm trying to say is we occasionally have to take a broader view. When was the last time you went to any of the settlements? Either in Jersey or Long Island?"

"A long time, not since I was little. We visited some friends of my parents one weekend. My mother always thought the settlements were wretched and filthy."

Peter's mother had forbidden his father from ever taking him there again. She was convinced he'd get sick if he spent too much time there.

"Once?" Richard asked. "They're very different, but they're full of regular people—people living in communities, getting by on what they can. Have you ever heard of the Highlands settlement?"

"Yes, by the Jersey shore," Peter said.

"Right. They have a few thousand folks living there. They usually subsist by hunting, some fishing and shelling, and some crops such as tomatoes, cabbages, root veggies for the winter."

"But they have the blight," said Sri. "The crops failed in the spring, and we don't have any stored for winter."

"At the same time, the deer disappeared. They used to have a controlled hunt a few times a year, but the entire herd has either died out or migrated to cooler areas. And, as you know, they can eat local sea flesh only once a week or risk poisoning."

"So they're having trouble with their food supply?" Peter asked.

"No, Peter, they're starving. They're desperate. So do you understand now?"

"No, because the *Muni 14* will dump the kelp in one of the infected zones.

How does that help the Highlands?"

"Ah, that's the complicated part. The short story is that they won't dump the kelp. Not most of it, at least."

"They'll stop at the Highlands? They have a dock and a processing plant?"

"No, that's the complication. The *Muni 14* will leave the bay and anchor offshore until nightfall. Then, if the ocean is calm enough, they'll try to transfer the kelp onto a local boat fleet. It's very hard, very dangerous."

Peter leaned back into his chair. "So it's not just you then? The deckhands are also a part of this conspiracy?"

"It's not a conspiracy. It's—"

"I must disagree, sir! It *is* a conspiracy. You're falsifying records, breaking your oath, and involving different departments." Peter had never raised his voice to Richard before.

"Peter, please. I need you to see the bigger picture. Our Manhattan kelp supplies have been overflowing since we switched fields a few months ago. If we didn't get another shipment for six months, we'd still be able to supply the entire island. Yet the people in the Highlands will starve to death if we don't help them."

After a long pause, Peter sighed. "It seems noble enough. I wish the best for the people in the Highlands and everywhere else. But we have a duty, a sworn oath to protect and nourish the people on this island. And, like my father always said, principles are black and white. It's a slippery slope when we abandon them."

Richard slumped back into his chair.

Peter pushed away from the table and grabbed his clipboard. "I'm afraid you leave me no choice, Head Inspector. As the second most senior inspector, I must report you to the liaison. The *Muni 14* is probably still at the Brooklyn Fuel Depot for their weekly allotment of diesel. The liaison can still order it back." He then walked out of Richard's office.

"Peter, wait! Please." Richard strode past Peter and turned to block his way. "Okay, okay, I get it. This violates our ethics. It's not ideal. But, please, let's slow down. There are some things—"

"Richard, sir, I've heard enough."

"No, you haven't. Stop."

Peter's eyes widened, but he stopped.

"This isn't an abstract thing," Richard said. "Look around at our fellow department members. Where do you think they live? They don't live with us on the Fresh Kills Heights. They live in the settlements. Many of them live in the Highlands."

Peter glanced at the men in red.

"Really look at them, Peter. They're our colleagues. We've worked with them for years, and they are in trouble. Can't we help them? Can't we say that they're as important as a banker? When they go home tonight, their families won't have enough food. Imagine if you couldn't bring food home to your parents. What would happen to them?"

"Well, as part of our job," Peter said, "we can bring back food."

"*You* can bring back enough food for your mother to cook dinner for you every night, but that doesn't work for thousands of Muni workers."

"Your mother cooks for you every night? With department food?" asked Sri.

"I hear your point," Peter said, "but where does it stop, Richard? What happens next?"

Peter stepped around Richard and walked out of the silent room. Richard and Sri followed him as Augie, lingering by the office door, joined the group.

The three men trailed Peter into the stairwell as he lumbered to the fourth floor, toward the liaison meeting room. The lights flickered on.

"Ah, perfect timing," Peter said. "We have power. The liaison must be here."

Augie pushed past Peter and placed his left arm across the door. His other arm hung stiffly behind his back.

"There are two more things you should know before you report me to the liaison," said Richard.

Peter looked through the glass panel in the door and saw the brightly lit hallway leading to the conference room. The room held a long, narrow table surrounded by six chairs. A man and a woman in red coveralls straightened the chairs and placed a carafe of water on the table.

"It appears the meeting hasn't started," Peter said. "And since you're blocking the way, you might as well proceed."

Richard stood in front of Peter and placed a hand on his shoulder. Peter winced.

"You need to know that this isn't the first time we've redirected a shipment of kelp to a settlement." Richard nodded his head as he spoke.

"I'm not sure that makes this any better. In fact, it would mean that this is a long-running conspiracy."

"Good lord, enough with the conspiracy nonsense. We've done it for years. *Years.*"

The three men watched Peter. He squinted his eyes at Richard.

"How many years?" Peter asked.

"At least twenty. I'm not exactly sure."

"But you've been Head Inspector for only the past eight years."

Richard squeezed Peter's shoulder.

"That would mean ... my father...?"

Richard smiled tightly and gave a quick nod.

"Dad did this? He falsified inspections and sent good shipments away?"

Peter stepped back and grabbed the handrail. "I don't believe it. He couldn't have been part of this."

"It was P.A.-Two's idea," said Augie. "He knew what was happening in the settlements, said he wanted to help."

Peter looked at his feet and let out a low moan.

"He's a great man," said Augie. "He saved many lives."

In the meeting room, a tall, slender woman in a pantsuit sat at the head of the table. The woman in red coveralls walked toward the stairwell door and knocked on the window.

"It's time to meet with the liaison. I'm going in," said Richard. "Do you plan on coming too, Peter?"

Peter shook his head. "No, sir."

Augie stood aside, and Richard pulled open the door.

Before the Head Inspector could step into the hallway, Peter said, "What was the other thing? You said there were two things."

"It's not important now. We'll talk about it later." Richard let go of the door and walked down the hallway and into the conference room.

Peter sniffled and walked down the stairs. Sri and Augie watched him turn the corner.

Sri looked at Augie and exhaled. "Can I give this to you?" He held out a steel pipe he had kept hidden in his coveralls.

"Yup." Augie took the pipe with his free hand and pulled an oversized screwdriver from behind his back.

As the ferry approached the dock at Fresh Kills Heights, Peter stood and grabbed his bag of food. Richard followed him as he stepped off the boat and lumbered down the dock wedged between two methane stacks.

The two men in yellow stopped in front of a tall, lean man with the same curly hair as Peter's and a thin man with a long grey beard, loose green pants, and a faded sweatshirt.

Peter dropped the bag of food at the tall man's feet and slumped his shoulders.

Peter Arbuckle II grabbed the bag. "Is everything all right?" He looked at his son, then at Richard.

"Everything's okay now," Richard said. "I think you and Peter have a long night ahead of you."

Peter's father put his arm around his son and walked toward the steep steps that led into the village. Peter rested his head on his father's shoulder.

The bearded man pointed toward the empty ferry. "So do we, brother, so do we...."

Jonathan Reif

Hot Chips

E VERY DAY, AFTER SCHOOL, the boys would meet at the school's entrance. From
there we walked together for a bit, we're slapping each other around as we
go, just some casual sparring, usually picking on someone. But as each kid
went home their own way, the group gradually shrank, and the rest of us would
continue.

Eventually, it was just me and him. I thought he was a nice kid, bit of a
scrawny geek, but a nice kid, and I wouldn't touch him. We would chat about
some sport or whatever until we came to our local neighborhood store, a real
grease factory, and he would always go in. I waited outside for him. He came
out with the same thing every day, some disgusting, greasy hot chips. I guess
you would call them French fries?

Every day after school the same thing. We would then walk in silence the
rest of the way. Well, he would be noisily slurping down his oily chips, while
walking, completely concentrated on them, and I'm right beside him not saying
a word. But they were way too greasy. A chip is supposed to be crunchy. His
soggy chip drooped, dripping with oil, as he held it in his fingers above his
mouth, head tilted back as he's walking along, but eyes closed as he's slurping it
down in one go. Each one goes down the same way. Without a word he would
carry on like this. Never a single glob of chip left as I departed down my avenue
and he carried on licking up whatever awful chip-oil soup remained.

I can't repeat myself often enough on this point. Every day, we walked home
and he would get his hot chips from our grubby corner store and I was there
as he ate. Now what if I were to say to you that not one single day in all that
time did this kid offer me a single hot chip? Not once. I walk home with this
guy every day and we're friendly. He wasn't my best friend in school, sure, that
point I will concede, but we were two of the guys. We got along well. So don't
you think you would at least once, just one time I ask you, ask your friend,

45

"would you like a chip?" You don't even have to ask, just nudge the chips at me, give me a nod, and then I can make the call, either take a chip or politely decline, "No thanks." Either way, it would be civil and humane just to ask once, or even every now and then. "Would you like one?" "Please, help yourself to one of my hot, possibly even tasty, chips."

But not a single time was this offer made. I walk with this kid every day. We have a bond, not the strongest of bonds, but there is a connection. Would it have been too much if this kid could have just once asked me if I would like one? It was infuriating.

So one day after school, we're walking along as usual. This kid comes out with his damn hot chips again. I honestly don't even care anymore. But there he is walking out, and there is a step down a couple of paces from the store entrance and for some reason he is not really paying attention. I am not sure if he ever paid attention. You should have seen the concentration in this kid as he dives into his silly chips. But he misjudges it this time, the step down, and he is about to gulp down one of those grease sticks right as he's coming out, it is about to land in his mouth, but he trips, I don't know how, at that very moment that he was stepping down, as if the step wasn't even there. He goes flying and so do his chips. He is now sprawled face down on the path. The kid is completely flat and horizontal, and his chips are then lying there scattered on the ground in all directions in front of me, some on the path, some in the dirt, maybe some on road.

And I am standing right there. It was beautiful. There are these disgusting chips scattered around, he is face down, and all is once more good and righteous with the world. Is there an English word for *Schadenfreude*? Never ever did get a single chip out of him.

One issue regards my father, but before that, allow me to say a few words about my grandfather, and maybe even my great-grandfather. My father's story is mildly tragic, but some context is always required or otherwise I feel you will judge him unfairly.

My great-grandfather was born toward the end of one of the great wars of the previous century. Is it mild serendipity that my great-grandfather was born on the same day as, in my humble opinion, the finest United Nations Secretary-General that I can recall in Ban Ki-moon, the man with the silver touch and the golden tongue? I wrote a paper on his methods back in school, and some of the treaties to halt global warming that he personally helped negotiate were never again bettered.

My great-grandfather's story is more humble than that of the magnificent Ban Ki-moon, but no less impressive to be honest. This is hard to understand now, but the aim of everyone back then was to retire happily ever after. What this means is a magical world full of cruise ships, around-the-world trips, golf … heaven on Earth as a country club. A cruise ship is like a large yacht, only with a more impressive buffet. This is a world of which even the best diplomats of today could only dream. My great-grandfather never reached or even came close to the post of Secretary-General, but the important point is that he worked the same job every day of his working life and retired at the age of sixty years. Pure Nirvana if you ask me. He was in retirement for almost as long as he had worked. Can you believe that?

I don't care what he did and it doesn't matter anyway. I would also do that if I could retire at the age of sixty. I'm not known to be squeamish, am I?

My grandfather was also pretty lucky. Moved around between various careers, never really finding his niche, I was told, but working hard and putting enough away to retire at about seventy. Not bad.

My father, though, is where that sort of luck runs out. He never missed a single day of work, I think. Sickness never prevented him from getting up every single day, driving the hour or so to whatever job, coming home late, and collapsing on the couch. Always working weekends. Hell, what's a weekend, anyway? And so he changed jobs many times, grinding for one company, then for their direct competitor, and then back again. It is all just musical chairs but he was always ready if the grass turned greener, as they say.

But he knew what he wanted, which was to retire happily ever after like his father and his father's father. Escape the cursed rat race. So the man was a precocious saver. Frugality is something I can admire. Even as a young man, he was an advocate of extreme early retirement. But with his earnings, he really couldn't afford to retire before the age of eighty years and still maintain his standard of living. Now he didn't make it to the age of eighty, but one can only admire the commitment and dedication to frugality throughout all those years, clinging to the dream.

So much for the background info. I think you know where this is going now, don't you?

So this one day, right, I am already up early because the folks are fighting again. It was definitely about money. Frugality was not one of my mother's strong points. Married up in class and probably expected to have had a better go of it. Maybe not even work herself, but like I said, we can all dream, right?

My aim almost every morning, or even the night before if he wasn't too sour—timing is everything, you see—was to score a couple of bucks off the father before he left. I was not fussy. Each day, it went something like this: Me: "So…" He: "Yes?" Me: "How 'bout it?" He: "How 'bout what?" Me: "Can I get a little something for the day?" He: "I gave you something yesterday." This was true, he did give me something yesterday; I could usually get something from him. It is just that inflation seemed to hit our family, and myself in particular, the hardest.

But on this day, he wasn't interested, didn't even respond gruffly, and simply walked past me out the front door. I always thought this was a useful game to teach me the value of money before handing me over a little something. A very responsible parenting sort of thing and something I can only admire to this day. But that day he wasn't having any of it, looking right through me—he was already out the door. I was now panicking because it was only morning and I was already hungry. But what are you gonna do?

Luckily in class at the time we were learning about the Tiananmen Square protests of 1989. I should be careful what I say here, but I remembered the image of one protestor stopping the progress of a tank with nothing but the force of his moral courage, or so it was taught to us. Of course, the use of tanks seems a bit excessive to us nowadays since protestors are easily dispersed with the strategic deployment of a few rayguns. So I went out there trailing him and stood behind his parked car so he couldn't reverse into the street. Well, he could reverse, but he would have had to roll over me in order to reach the street.

Of course he was screaming at me to get out the way. Something about being late for work and no time for silly games. Here I admit to feeling guilty about being possibly responsible for his being late for work for the first time ever. But I had invoked the spirit of Tiananmen Square and did not waver, remaining calm with my arms outstretched in righteous moral defiance. It was also made clear that I would move out the way if a few coins of hard currency were thrown out the window. One thing that occurred to my father but not to late-twentieth-century Chinese tank drivers, is that a slowly rolling vehicle is enough to nudge protestors gradually out of the way or even backward if it should be required. In fairness, if you are some peasant sitting in a tank, you have probably a limited political perspective and no training on how to handle civilians confronting tanks. What if that is your high school history teacher out there? But my father was more efficient in these matters.

He was reversing his car slowly toward me but no way was I going to dive under the wheels. You will be surprised to learn that a single human, and I was a relatively young human then, can impede the progress of a light, fuel-efficient vehicle before it is able to pick up sufficient speed. So I am shocked to find that I'm able to hold him and his little hatchback there with my strength alone, and his wheels begin to spin as he tries to reverse harder. He was frugal, but no doubt my father wished at that point that he had selected the next model up with slightly higher torque. Or is this just a question of traction? At any rate, it was somewhat of a groundbreaking day for me, self-confidence-wise. From that day on, and particularly on that day in question, I gained a new belief in my physical strength, which seemed to overflow into the rest of my development in other areas. You see, from my perspective, I'm not holding back some insipid fuel-efficient hatchback, but rather it is the might of a military tank that I am resisting.

Now mother has reentered the picture. How would that have looked from the kitchen window, your husband trying to reverse over your boy early one morning? She is outside now and coming toward us, screaming at father, flinging wedding and engagement rings at the windscreen—which did the trick. This forced my father to stop and check the damage to the windscreen, and I think mother has stormed immediately back inside. Even in those days getting a windscreen repaired was no small financial outlay and I could understand his chagrin at having to fork out even more resources. At that point, my father and I are both around the front of the car inspecting his windscreen, looking for damage. Lucky for us, those rings were far from diamonds and his windscreen escaped relatively unscathed. Another prudent choice from the old man, I thought, not investing in expensive wedding rings. But despite the near miss, my father is still distraught, a bit strung out, and even looks physically sick. I wonder whether this is his first ever day of missing work?

Even so, I was slightly shocked as mother comes flying out the door once more, and she jumps in the car while both father and I are still perusing the windscreen for damage. She closes the door and just reverses and drives off, and my father and I can only stand there, watching her go. I realize at that point that he is completely vulnerable. I am back in negotiating mode, trying to scrounge hard currency from the old scrooge. And of course he gives me a small amount without any resistance. Here I can highlight another point in my development. Make your opponent as vulnerable as possible, both before and even during negotiations. If things are changing on the ground during negotiations, all the better—your opponent starts to panic and make hasty and probably irrational decisions.

Of course, I did not realize it at the time. It was otherwise a completely uneventful day, although I am now feeling a foot taller, and walking around like I own the place. No one was slapping me around that day. It was actually only later in the day when I was almost completely starved that I realized it. I'm with my best friend and had just finally got that day's meal. I am holding these stupid hot chips, I think you would call them French fries—good cheap food high in calories—ready to finally quench my hunger, when it occurs to me that this is likely the end of my parents' marriage, which, unfortunately, was the exact moment I trip on this step outside the store that I would have negotiated every single school day prior to that one without fault. And there I am, lying face down in the dirt without having consumed even a single chip before they too had also hit the dirt.

I hope this helps?

☉

So it turns out, go figure, that it is this cheap selfish chip kid who is now finance minister. The finance minister, who never once offered me a hot chip in all those years, has decided to raise the age of retirement. The official retirement age now exceeds the average life expectancy! What sort of sick "reform" is that?

Now I work hard. I work on call, every day. I put up with clueless management who blame everyone else when something doesn't work. I put up with slacker co-workers who don't do their job so I always have to step in. I deal with rude customers who don't ever know what they want, and I have to pry their problems out of them and then solve those problems for them. Why do they always force these guys on me? I don't ever take a sick day. Never take time off. Have never even asked for a raise and barely take a lunch break.

But I keep at it, because I know eventually it's all gonna pay off. I'll finally get to retire blissfully, I'll give my boss the finger, I'll tell my co-workers to go to hell, and then I'll take it easy. Finally get all those jobs done around the house, maybe visit some old friends. Except him of course.

So one day I am working a double shift again. I have just rid myself of another witless customer. I have not even eaten all day, I'm starving—and then news comes in that the government is raising the official age of retirement. And there he is on the screen, the honorable finance minister himself, speaking to the media. And watching it, I suddenly realize they are filming just a short distance away. And that is when I decide I'm finished for today, and I'm gonna go see him. I am *not* angry. I just want to speak to him.

I get in my car, methodically, and drive very sensibly—under the speed limit— until I reach downtown. I can already see from the main street the cluster of media there and so I figure he should be somewhere in the middle. It is pretty crowded, so I figure I can just sort of push my way through. I remember even discussing this very strategy with the now finance minister on one of those school days while we were walking home. I think we were learning about the 1989 Tiananmen Square protests and we agreed it was possible that those tanks could have just nudged the protestors out the way without harming anyone while saving face politically.

And so I was trying to execute the same thing here. I'm driving slowly and pushing through people a bit but most of them are getting out of the way by themselves. But then security is trying to get the finance minister away, so I have to speed up a bit to catch him.

As usual the cops overreact, and they're now dragging me, violently I might add, out of my car, calling me a terrorist. I ain't no terrorist. I pay my taxes, man. But I manage to wrestle free briefly and get over towards him. But I can't think of anything quickly to say to him, and so I'm just like, "GIVE ME A CHIP, MAN! GIVE ME SOME CHIPS!!!" That is why I said that.

Jeff Burt

Squatting

M<small>Y WIFE AND</small> I left Chicago after forty-five years. Both sixty-three, we had lost our jobs, our house, and then our apartment. I had been a carpenter who had worked at the McCormick Center for trade shows and expositions, and a working manager the last twenty years, and now was an exhibit for the early demise of the body—my knuckles bulged with bursitis, fingers misshapen from breaks and hammer hits, knees swollen and legs bowed like parentheses. We were too young for Medicare. Health insurance did not pay the rent, food stamps and Second Harvest did not quite cover the food, and we had grown tired of holding out our hands at every church trying to get the utilities paid and a few bus passes. We weren't poor. We were barbarous, scrounging in culverts and gutters, not afraid of disease or rats.

We left with two backpacks and one large grey duffel bag, took a bus up I-90, and stepped off in the dark around eight P.M. on a roundabout outside of Hartford, Wisconsin. We kept stepping until we found an old farmhouse with no lights on and no yard light coating the golden crushed gravel of the barn lot, a sagging roof, and a chimney a few bricks shy of complete, about as much as we could tell by flashlight. Our intent was to squat.

Without a car we could own and maintain, each stop accommodated death, because motion is living, having the potential to move is hope. By squatting, we meant to die.

I could just as well have kicked the bucket, but Evelyn, a woman of belief, had no faith in her promised hereafter. She held to every second of life.

In death there is no dignity, and usually not in the dying, either. We slow-cook until we fall apart like pulled chicken or a hunk of beef charred and done up in seconds. An old man passes in a diaper. An old woman curses, yells you are trying to kill her. Already Evelyn at times could not recall my name. Already Evelyn, a most organized person, slipped into dementia and disorganization, mental chaos gripping her and pulling her down into a swirling sea of ignorance and enemies.

Unlike many young squatters, we were not running away needing space, but running toward the absence of space. It wasn't stability we desired, but suspension, like a spider that starts to slide down his silky filament but stops to review exactly where it is he will land, where he will stay: a moment when he can decide what to do next with clarity.

But clocks tick and the wind blows and the spider that halts is carried to an unexpected place. We had stopped. We had stepped off. We wanted a roof over our heads, even walls closing in on us, and this old farmhouse at the end of town at the end of a long and Jordan River–like road suited us.

Evelyn and I had practiced squatting for several weeks in Chicago before we set out. We had occupied a small apartment in a three-story in Evanston near Northwestern University. Evelyn had fallen in love with the vegetable garden in the rear, even dusted with snow. The simple knowledge that she could enjoy something green elated her, even though we were not staying. The ivy, also dormant, twined all the way to the second story, where we squatted. We could not use the heat, but were fortunate to be on the second floor. The temperature sank to forty-five at night, and rose to fifty-two in the day, never less, never more, and we found that sharing a sleeping bag, sleeping around the clock, and reading, we could survive. But the apartment invited fear—we found quickly that we were afraid to talk, that conversation would alert our neighbors and they would kick us out. So we learned a great repertoire of pantomimes for telling the other we were going to the bathroom, or bathing, or that we needed to go to the store. Eventually we had enough confidence to light a fire in the wood stove in the corner of the kitchen near the windows facing west and north, but we only spoke in whispers.

We learned a valuable lesson in our trial: if we were going to squat, and we were, we needed a house so we could speak to each other. We had also learned that most people don't care who moves in or out next door, and don't intend to interact. Ever. Meet-and-greets and welcome mats are relics of the past. The future lay in forced nods of acknowledgement and furtive glances.

In the first night, I used the toilet and the water worked, and the lights turned on, though we only flashed them for a second.

In the morning, I searched the pantry but it was bare. The house had been cleaned to sell some time ago, and when I ran a finger across a counter, I accumulated enough dust that it fell off my finger. But the house had beauty. The old doors, solid wood, had browned to a light chocolate, and had been oiled to keep the resin sealed in. Several china cabinets made of boxwood shone with that soft yellow patina that glows in morning sunlight, and the pulls and handles were of a grade of metal that did not flake or oxidize.

The oven had a leak—the gasket was missing four inches of seal, but as we would use it as a warmer, that did not bother me.

The refrigerator gleamed, stainless steel, the newest item in the house. Still powered; the air inside, though stale, smelled of cleaning powder, chlorine. When I shut the door, the condenser came on, and with it, that sick groan a door makes when it is not level, when the hinge hangs unevenly and the rubber washer rucks and rumples to one side, echoes and sounds its alarm, as if alerting someone in the house that another has raided the fridge.

The bathtub and sink were made of iron, so never warmed, no matter the steam and the wrinkling that occurred when I took a bath. The pipes were rusty and had stained the tub and sink with what looked like the blots psychiatrists use to dig into your id. I did not have much of an id anymore, so the blots looked like rust blots to me. The kitchen water tasted of iron, but when I let the water run long enough it cleared up. The pipes clacked and sounded more like geese telling me to go away, then with one mighty belch went mute. A rich assortment of dull silver appliances sat on the counter, as if pouting from lack of use. When I tried the toaster, the right slot's lever didn't spring, a fuse clicked off, and I could smell the tang of burning wire. The linoleum, cracked and yet relaxed, had a thin scrim of dust. The wood floor of the dining room had a few chips and splits and could have used a fresh coat of oil or wax. The wallpaper, which would once have been thought garish with its large dahlia print, now appeared modern, though a little darkened by time.

The farmhouse had newer bedrooms built around the old kitchen and living room and the family room was modern, network-adapted, with a hole for a large-screen hi-def TV. But take one step from the family room into the old, and the drafty, uninsulated floors took hold, and wool socks and shit-kicking boots were a requirement. The civility of the room changed as well, into the common cursing and cussing of a kitchen, heard in the wounds of the linoleum, the nicks on the cupboards, and the splintered doorpost. Caesar had his Rubicon, this family had their kitchen threshold. The kitchen only warmed in the morning with the eastern light, so I shut the doors to the living room and never opened them again.

Outside, in the back by the barn and the sheds, the paint seemed alive, the ground yielded, as it should in the spring, full of melt. I expected pigs, donkeys, chickens scattered and pecking, stray cats drooling in the hay by the dugs of cows, heads in stanchions, but the barn had mold, fungus, and the smell of gasoline as if a vehicle had recently been parked inside. The animals were long gone, perhaps sold at auction or to neighbors.

⊙

Sarah James, wide-eyed and wearied, fourteen, stood outside the convenience store, a no-name place once a 7-11 then downscaled into half a liquor store and half snacks, coffee and Slurpees, run by two brothers who were overly polite. She was waiting for her boyfriend and thinking of her life in the valley, her nothingness through high school, as if she was a blot of ink spilled on paper, or an anonymous growth on the side of a beautiful tree, and now her adulthood had taken on the same formlessness—a job at minimum wage working alongside similar people with similar lives that dished on music and parties and recipes and sex, but had no deposits in the bank of the future. She was waiting for her boyfriend, twice her age, chiseled not by workouts but by prison and sleeping on the floors of ten friends over the past five years, a boyfriend who wooed her, and when he talked looked straight into her eyes, and then kept looking into her eyes the entire conversation. He came flying out the door with blood on one hand and cash in the other, a lot of blood, a little cash, and her old life evaporated. When the wheels squealed at the exit it was equaled by the silent shriek in her heart, a shriek of gladness, of opportunity, of escape, and she too ran to his car.

I grabbed her before she could get in. I can't tell you why. Just like a mother holding a toddler can break a fall with her own body to make sure the baby isn't injured, sacrificing herself and the natural inclination of DNA to save oneself, I grabbed her.

I held her by the back of the jacket, then wrestled with her as she hit me to get free, then gave her a bear hug, until the tire squealing faded from our ears and fresh sirens from the cops came forward.

I kept telling her she'd be fine as she became boneless in my arms, wilted, Evelyn patting her on the back, stroking back and forth, up and down, as if she could fill every open pore, each one a wound, with the salve of simple fingertips and palms.

The cops asked a few questions, but Sarah had not entered the store, so she had committed no crime except in her heart, which, if you listen to Evelyn, is the same in terms of your soul, but, I reminded her, not in the consequences of life.

I lied to the cops, which Evelyn winked at, which meant we'd have a row later on.

"She's my granddaughter. Got terrified when the man ran out. First time she's seen a gun."

Sarah was homeless, a runaway from Minneapolis, a runaway from her single mother, a runaway from school where she couldn't focus, a runaway from feeling fat, a runaway from being poor, a runaway from texting and Facebook where no one texted or liked back. When I asked her if she had ever run toward something, she whispered, "Yes, once, and you grabbed me."

She came with us, refusing to talk to me, hand in hand with Evelyn. We took a few shortcuts to stay off the streets, made sure we cut through a back lot at the edge of town, and then stayed behind the garage for about fifteen minutes before sliding around the back of the house and going in.

We had food, a bag of brown rice, a bag of beans, an enormous block of cheese, and two bags of day-old bread, plus an assortment of canned food and cinnamon-swirl coffee cakes that had been donated to Second Harvest. The kicker, though, was fruit and vegetables: fresh, small apples and navel oranges, broccoli and celery, and a few thick-skinned onions and a few pounds of potatoes. Evelyn had swiped a tub of salsa, too, which would go great on the potatoes.

Sarah was happy to share, too. She had strawberry Fruit Roll-ups, chocolate-covered blueberries, a half-eaten bag of tortilla chips that had become ground dust in her jacket, and three packets of instant coffee. We started with the instant coffee. It tasted horrible, but it was a good horrible.

We got along. I didn't try to give Sarah any advice. Evelyn had enough proverbs for both of us. But they came out of her mouth with a gentleness that surprised. It was easier to talk to a child when you were a grandparent, it seemed. The battle or contention for a place in the sun had vanished. We were old, no threat to her ego. We didn't have to sound parental; we didn't have to sound wise. We only had to sound like grandparents who loved her, but whose egos her outcome was no longer attached to.

Squatter's not a nice term. Some may think it smacks of ingenuity, adventure, using unused resources in a new way. It is none of those. It means you've occupied where you do not have a legal right, that you are doing something illegal. There's no moral high ground on that definition.

But squatting implies, well, squatting, and squatting is not like kneeling, where there is a sense of honor left in the humiliation, and an outcome of restoration at some point. No, one squats to take a shit in a hole or a latrine. One squats to squeeze a cow's dugs with one's face right next to the shitting ass of it. One squats to pick up what's dropped. One squats to reason with a child, but in squatting, places oneself at the level of the child. A baseball catcher squats, the dirtiest job in baseball, one prone to injury. They always talk about the intelligence of a catcher, but the greatest intelligence is to be better at another position, and any catcher will leave catching to play first base. Old, downsized, and drained out of the economy like morsels that fit through the trap in the sink and are whisked into the sewer, we had met the ceiling of our intelligence, and it belonged to someone else.

☉

On the second day Evelyn, Sarah, and I bee-lined it for a flea market on the vacant lot next to a closed grocery store. I say bee-lined it because we didn't have the energy to meander, so much of our walking was a straight line to and from some appointed place.

Everyone was selling used stuff, spoons from places like Flagstaff and Tuscaloosa that were so small a tongue could wrap around them, umbrellas with taped handles for a buck that a hard rain would dash into quarters, video games in their plastic sleeves and some without, fewer and fewer books. It seemed in one generation the reading public had contracted like a pond in a hot summer.

"I should sell something," I said. "So should you. Raise a few bucks."

"I've got nothing."

"Me either."

"I've got my mother's good looks," Evelyn laughed.

"Hell, my face wouldn't get a dime. I, however, could do a portrait with ink on my elbow which looks like Abraham Lincoln."

"Maybe they'd want the actual elbow."

"That would cost them extra, but I would make it available," I said.

"What about the sweat from my brow?"

"Now you're thinking."

Evelyn drew two fingers across her forehead. "And the wisdom in my wrinkles."

I said, "The temples of my head have been seldom visited. See. A smooth pate."

"Same thing for my mind. Virtually unused," she said.

"Ah, that brings up another thing to sell. Memories."

"I don't have too many of those, and you need to keep what you have for me," she responded.

"I should sell the notes that I sing, start with the long ones for the most cash."

"And the short ones?" she asked.

"The shorter the notes the less I can get. It takes many short notes to equal a long one. And I might not have enough room in the basket."

"You might just sell the basket. I've heard you sing, and the basket could be worth a lot more," she said.

"But I need to keep the basket for the notes."

"Then you won't sell a thing."

"I know. Depressing, isn't it," I said.

"We all want gold," Evelyn said, "but when it comes down to it, a shiny copper suffices." She proceeded to remove a shiny debit card and paid.

☉

Dementia sounds like a Greek goddess, and she is when you have it, the cold bearings of your fists containing contraband stolen from your own cupboard when you weren't looking, she with flowing gown and arms raised in either applause or boredom, her elegant ankles crossed as if she were ascending into the filtered light because all light is filtered when you're demented, and things rise, like when I was standing in Brazos County, Texas, and a dust devil formed and my eyes rose from the tail to the spinning top loosened like the gown of my woman ready to fall from her breasts and I stood there and watched until it rose over the top of me and threw me to the ground and disappeared. I rose jarred and pissed off, dusted off, and came to my senses. Evelyn doesn't always dust herself off any more, doesn't always come to her senses. Often she will stay in bed most of the day afraid to rise, so I was happy that she was mentally with me this day, full of repartee. It was not often any longer that the boy she met on Lakeshore Drive met the girl she was on Lakeshore Drive, but when we did, it made the years melt and under a snow of miscomprehension, of dementia, was the original sidewalk of our love.

It took a day for Sarah to enter into conversation, to let her cell phone go idle, to get off the floor where she sat next to an outlet so she could recharge the battery of her phone, an every-three-hour operation. What sparked her involvement was a simple word: haircut. I needed one. I was not comfortable with Evelyn cutting my hair any longer, and had trouble doing it myself. So when Sarah jumped to her feet willing to snip, I took her up on it.

I warned her as we searched for appropriate linen to wrap around my torso that wild hairs sprouted on my neck like thistles standing alone in a field cropped short by grazing cows, and my moles were dark like moist mounds elevated by gophers digging caverns down below.

"I'm all grinds and bumps, scaled like a green snake to slither, camouflaged on my forearms with spots they kindly call aging, the page of my youth having turned some time ago."

"Oh, you're not so bad. I've seen worse. I cut my brother's hair, and he had some pretty gnarly warts."

"Ah, warts. I have avoided those. But my triceps sag, my biceps buckle, my left shoulder from a slide into second base slumps as if air alone is too heavy a burden to bear, and my neck bows finally but grudgingly humble."

"Well piss and shit, grandpa, you're old. You're supposed to be like that."

She did a wonderful job, wetting me down first, then pulling up my hair every inch or so and snipping an even line. She was deft with the comb and scissors, more than I imagined for a fourteen-year-old. She had confidence that belied her neediness.

"Can I trim your beard," she started, and then sensing my hesitance, "just the sides and towards the bottom of your neck?"

I nodded my acceptance, but watched very closely as the gray hairs fell to the linen.

Evelyn said she had done a fine job, and gave her a mirror to hold in front of my face.

"My best haircut in years," I said, "but I'm wearing bifocals and can't quite see for sure."

"He hates his bifocals," Evelyn chirped. "One of the unintended consequences of bifocals, he told me, is that men reach the wrong conclusion in the neighboring stall of the urinal when he keeps shifting his head up and down and side to side trying to read the graffiti on the walls."

Sarah laughed.

Sarah removed the linen and shook it out the back door, then returned and swept up the trimmings with her bare hand.

I offered her ten dollars but she pushed it back.

"It's my gift," she said, and then returned to her cell phone. Now she was happy and talkative.

Sarah's boyfriend made bail in three days, and found us on the fourth. I remember him like broken glass, sharp, irregular, with a glint in the sunlight that pierced and almost made me turn away, but his words seemed worn, as if washed and dulled by a bad childhood, the shine taken off. I felt sorry for him, so depressed in speech and yet so hard-edged in tone and frame. But not sorry enough that I was going to let Sarah go off with him.

I could tell when he'd face me that he was looking to see if I was still strong enough to fend him off, so I took to glaring, showing the whites of my eyes, which also had a lot of red in them from blood vessels that had almost popped many a time. It seemed to work. He became consigned and conciliatory by dark, and wanted to hang around for dinner and then leave.

We ate ravioli from a few cans and carrots and some hunks of cheese, which Sarah wolfed down, and then it was dark, a beautiful dark, warmer than it should have been. We went outside in the back and peered through the gauzy interference of a mist, hunting for meteor showers the paper had mentioned, like paparazzi thirsty for a shot of a movie star on media tour. Evelyn called out one I never saw, and Sarah picked up on that but kept exclaiming how lucky Evelyn was to see ones we didn't, which pleased Evelyn like she was a child, all puffed up and proud. What I did not miss was her eager face caught in perpetual ease and anticipation, her eyes in constant motion because no friction between this world and the next could slow them down, her energy conserved and yet exhausted as we lay on the field with a thousand exploding shards of space in the small sparkle left on the grass and branches of light in the sky.

We stayed outside while Sarah and her boyfriend went to say a final good-bye, and then I heard Sarah scream.

When I entered the house, Ronnie was dumping Sarah's backpack and purse on the floor, and had already dumped Evelyn's purse. He was frantic. When he saw my boots, he looked up like a dog that was about to be kicked, contorting his body about halfway up to yield to the boot.

But I didn't kick him. I pulled him up by his ears, took him to the door, and watched him walk sideways from the house down the driveway like a coyote, slide into his faded red Sentra, rev the motor, and leave.

Evelyn was comforting Sarah, both on their knees, as Sarah scooped up her papers and belongings and stuffed them back in her bags.

"Dear, he didn't get your money or your cards. I took them before he came. I've hidden them in my dress," she cooed, giving them back. "When we meet strangers, I always hide mine in my dress and Walter's wallet, too. I've had them since before we went outside. I've been sitting on them. No one checks the back of the panties, you know."

Sarah laughed and gave her an air hug.

Ten minutes later Evelyn handed Sarah the debit card and my driver's license and my wallet, thinking Sarah had been sent to confiscate them. She insisted that Sarah take the cards to the point of becoming violent. Sarah fought back, twisting Evelyn's right arm and using her weight, chest-bumping Evelyn back against the wall. I put myself between them, but I had to restrain Evelyn with an almost suffocating hug.

It took another ten minutes for Evelyn to return to her sweet self. But those twenty minutes had opened a different world to Sarah, and I saw fear in how often her hand pushed food into her mouth, how eagerly she ate, how astonishingly animated she had become.

"She have a stroke or something?"

"No," I said, trying to be monotone, hoping the lack of a chromatic scale might reassure Sarah. "She has episodes, not in her right mind."

"How often? A lot?"

"Once or twice a day. Harmless. Sometimes she becomes angry, like today. Sometimes she becomes a four-year old girl, incredibly sweet. In both cases, with very little signs of intelligence."

"She should be in a home. The government will pay for it."

"We have a home," I said, gesturing with a sweep of my arm, trusting that

Evelyn had simmered down enough I could hug her with only one arm. "This is our new home. She would vanish into a cloud if I wasn't with her, and I would vanish as well."

"That's sad," Sarah said without any note of disapproving or pronouncement, but with a strange and true sense of misery.

Sarah left on the seventh day. We weren't sure she was gone, since she carried everything she owned in her backpack and little travel bag hoisted over one shoulder. She didn't leave us a note, so I can't say she has a happy ending of being reunited with her mother, and we didn't feel very excited about her going back to her mother in the first place. We figured it out when we saw the granola bars missing, which was a joy to my teeth, since I was afraid to crack a tooth on one, and probably a windfall to her.

Evelyn had a cry in the dining room, such a dark room it seemed a perfect place to shed a tear. She said that Sarah had been receiving many texts, and replying to them quickly. She knew it was the boyfriend, one sick animal calling to another, she said.

The day after Sarah's departure, we saw neighbors down the road circulating near the house. We made sure we stayed away from windows, at one time hiding in an upstairs closet. By the time the cops came, we were already half a mile away. They stopped us, and we had a polite conversation, telling them we were headed to Chicago, that we knew people there, that our apartment had suffered damage and we had been evicted without a vehicle or a place to go. They bought it, or didn't care to perturb two old folks walking toward a dim future.

Evelyn cinched the escape by saying in a lilting voice, "We have no place to go but Chicago," as if it were a line from a musical, and she had entered dementia, but it was only her happy humor.

In the Hartford circular real estate section I found a farmhouse that was for sale, outside of Pewaukee, and discovered the house had been for sale for over three years. I looked at the satellite image of the farmhouse on a computer at the public library, and no other house was within a half a mile. It stood at the end of a long drive that took a ninety-degree turn at the end. Almost invisible. A place where Evelyn could park, and I could tinker. Spring was in full bloom, and I imagined we could make it through the summer.

David England

The Lore of Bread

"Why, greetings o' the Great Mother there, Skye! How are you a-doin' this fine day? Good to hear that, child, good to hear. I suppose since you're here that your momma and Aunt Jessie have headed off to the mill to get the crop o' wheat ground? Oh—don't worry yourself none about that—the two o' them'll be jus' fine. We haven't had bandits on that road for years now. The priestesses at the Moon Temple laid the law on those last 'uns. And the pickled man-parts are still a-hangin' up as warnin'. Trust me, little one, no man is fool enough to risk that part o' himself. Your ma and Jessie will be back in a day or so with a cart o' flour, jus' dependin' on who all's got to the mill afore them.

"Now you come on over here and help your Gramma. I'm gonna teach you some lore today. We're gonna get to makin' bread for bakin' come mornin'. This is Earth-lore, child, and you'd do well to pay attention.

"Remind me how old you are again, Skye? My! Seven whole summers! Yes, you are getting to be a fine young lady. You've been mindin' your prayers, haven't you? That's good, child. It's important to pay the gods proper respect; every grown-up in the village knows this. Always three, Skye. You be rememberin' that even if you've forgot all else: Lord Helion, Lady Selena, and the Great Mother. Now you take this here pitcher and fetch me water from the well. I'll start settin' out what we're gonna need.

"Back already? You are a fast one! Mind you, I had that kind of energy once, too, when I was a girl like you. These two-and-forty summers are slowin' me down just a bit. Oh, don't fret your head—your Gramma's got a ways afore the Great Mother calls me back to Her.

"Get me that there jar of honey, Skye, and the small crock o' salt. That salt comes special from the east, you know. Traders bring it on their boats to us all the way from the land of the rising sun, where the salt farmers work the tide-pools o' the Ocean and let the great Helion burn away the water to leave the salt behind.

"What's an Ocean, you ask? Why I've not seen it myself, mind you, but I've heard talk of it before. It's like the Shygan here—water so big and vast you can't see the other side—but even bigger. So big that it wraps around the whole world. And the water's not sweet like the Shygan, either, but salty, and the waves roll in all the time, not just when the wind is up.

"Now, get me that big bowl over there, Skye, an' we'll get to mixin' it all together. Flour, salt, and the honey. Always three, Skye. You remember that, child. Three's a special number, a magical number, that holds all the mystery of this life and the life on the other side of the veil. Always three. The sun for the day, the moon for the night, and the Earth for the Great Chalice that holds the world. Each lore has its place. That's one of the important things the Ancients forgot.

"Oh, the Ancients? Well, I'm sure you've heard some of the stories, though those are mostly to keep the younguns in line an' teach 'em good manners an' proper behavin'. But there's more to the lessons o' the Ancients than jus' child's tales. A whole lot more.

"Now some folks say the Ancients were evil. An' some think like the bards and the tutors of the temples, that they were fools who lost their way. And what do I think, you ask? I'll tell you, Skye: I think the Ancients were babies. Babies who didn't know any better, an' in that not-knowin' did some very bad things. You remember when your little cousin Seth tried to touch the candle-fire and his momma slapped his hand away afore he burnt himself? That's what I think the Ancients were like. Just like baby Seth, 'cept they had no momma to slap their hand away from the fire and so they ended up burnin' themselves, and burnin' the whole world.

"This looks good, Skye. We've got almost everything. Now there's jus' one more thing we need an' that's over there in the corner. See that jar with the cloth tied on top? Go get that for your Gramma.

"Thank you, child. This here's the heart o' the bread-lore. This here's the bread-mother. We'll pour it in the bowl, but not all, 'cause we need to save some to keep a-growin' for tomorrow's bread. There we go. Now stir it till it gets real thick an' then we'll start foldin' it over an' workin' in the herbs.

"You know, people are like that, too, Skye. They need to have the experience of life folded into them over and over again so that they can grow proper. Sometimes they get too puffed up with themselves too soon, before they're ready, like the Ancients did. When that happens, they get punched down good and hard so that things can get folded in some more. One thing you can be sure of, Skye, and that's that no matter how it may look to the likes o' you and me, the gods know what they're a-doin'. An' it's always best to let the gods be and not argue with 'em none. That's somethin' else the Ancients didn't learn.

"Now, add a scoop o' flour to the jar with the bread-mother an' fill it back up with water an' give it a good stir. You remember this, Skye—every single day you gotta feed your tomorrow. Forget that, then one day tomorrow comes an' it's all starved an' barren for lack o' care. An' then you're in a world o' hurt. Ain't nothin' that can be done at that point but put your head down an' push through the rough time o' buildin' up again. That's what the Ancients lost sight of, Skye. Takin' time to feed their tomorrows. They got too full o' themselves, got so caught up in their learnin' that they forgot to be smart, an' got to thinkin' the feedin' oughta take care of itself somehow, no matter how much they took for themselves in a day. Well, they learned the hard way what happens when a body falls into that sort o' foolishness, an' we work hard to remember that lesson so's we don't make the same mistakes the Ancients did. So you feed your tomorrow, an' pay attention to the ways you've been taught, an' give the gods proper respect. Then you'll make it through more often than not.

"We got a right nice dough here, so let's get the herbs so's to make this a tasty loaf. Now I want to say somethin' else to you, young lady. I know your momma's told you 'bout the ways of the womb; it's not like you haven't seen the rabbits and the goats and the sheep goin' about their business anyways. There are folk in this world who think we tell younguns like you too much about such things—the People of the Book and their One God, them that live up-river a ways, are like that.

"But you're a-gonna be settin' up your own hearth and home in another six or seven summers, so it's 'portant for you to know what's what well before that first night. And pickin' a husband out is one of the biggest choices a woman makes in her life, so take your time an' don't let anyone rush you none. If'n you want my advice, though, you'll keep an eye on young Matthias—I think he's got the makin's of a good man for you when the time comes. No, you don't need to be makin' any decisions yet, that's for hand-fastin' an' you've got some time yet. I'm jus' sayin' to start thinkin' 'bout things so's you're not makin' a rush of it all when the time comes an' you make your declarations at the Moon Temple gates.

"What are the folks o' the temples like? Well, you'll be a-gettin' to go to some o' the more particular ceremonies soon enough. You've seen the grand high rites of the Great Day and the Great Night, of course. Now that you've gotten to seven summers yourself, your Momma and Pa can be a-takin' you to some o' the other ceremonies that happen at other times o' the year. You'll get plenty o' chances to see the priests and the priestesses goin' about their work, trust me.

"Each temple has its mysteries, its lore. The Sun Temple, that's for war an' star-lore an' law—'ceptin' women's law, which goes to the Moon. The Moon Temple's for healin' an' birthin' an' such law that's pertainin' to womenfolk. Then there's the Earth Temple, the Great Mother. That there's deep magic, Skye,

Earth-magic an' spirit-healin' an' lore beyond knowin' for most folks. There are priests and priestesses of the Sun, and only one Sun-Priest. There are priests and priestesses of the Moon, and only one Moon-Priestess. But there are only priestesses of the Earth, and only one High Priestess.

"An' the lore o' the temples has different layers, like the layers in one o' your Gramma's special cakes. You've got the outer mysteries first. Them everyone gets to see, things like the high holy days o' the Great Day an' the Great Night. Then there's the inner mysteries. Those you get to take part in as you start to become an adult. You'll get to learnin' the first o' them soon, Skye, now that you've got seven summers behind you. Once you get the full dozen, you'll see as much as any grown-up outside the temple gets to see. Last, there's the hidden mysteries. Those are for the priests an' priestesses o' the temples alone, them an' the students who've pledged themselves.

"The work o' the temples? Oh, that work, it's of a different kind, Skye. Not special—jus' different. An' it takes a different kind o' person to be a member of a temple. There's no handfastin' or marriage-bindin', for one thing. No family-raisin', no householdin', an' no younguns. No, them o' the temple let all that go so that they can put their lives into their studyin' the mysteries.

"That's why the temples only allow so many people to join, you know. You have to pass the tests first, of course, but then one o' the temples has to have a spot open in their ranks. Why? Well, you jus' think about it, Skye. If too many people went into the temples, there wouldn't be enough people plantin' crops an' tendin' the herds an' makin' babies. Then what would happen to all the villages? You see, we all got our place in this world, Skye, and no one's place is any better or holier than anyone else's, no matter what fancy robes a body is a-wearin'. Makin' babies is jus' as holy to the Great Mother as studyin' the mysteries o' Her temple. Never let anybody tell you different.

"This here looks like it's got the makin's of a right nice loaf, Skye. You'll make a fine woman o' your own household someday. Let's jus' sprinkle a bit more flour here over the top an' 'round the sides there—that keeps it from stickin' as it rises—then we'll cover it with this here cloth. Very good. Now go put it back in the corner over there an' we'll let it go for a while. Then we'll be a-punchin' it down an' foldin' it over some more before lettin' it rise one more time. Then comes the cookin' afore first light tomorrow.

"But we've got a bit more time now. Why don't you go over an' see if Matthias needs help with any o' his chores? I hear tell they've got plenty of eggs come out o' their hen-house these days. Never hurts to help others, Skye, as you never know when you'll need help yourself. You run along an' leave me to tidy up. Oh, I'll be fine—don't you worry none. Jus' get yourself back here afore the afternoon gets too far along, 'cause we've got dinner to be a-cookin' yet for your Pa. An' give Matthias' mama the Great Mother's greetin's from me, you hear?"

G. Kay Bishop

Characters Written
in Blood and Milk

OR, 3015

Aldest ya-zo daien dis daium: shee gibbewey mee er bootch.
Gahstling bootch! Dey doo vum da Nugguzzun a da Nortlek-an.
All Gadishilluns habun sunkaina nugguzzun ya-baiumbai. Dis-
sun allawey vum da Oddawaddas, ya-mam! Dem dam tredas
neba tellun zakli weyer dey geddun, ya-but blendifok nobaatun
oddazeel vurr. Shee unry-al bish, mostaium, nut gibbewey nut-
tin zlungas laiv mbret stil in er buddi. Ya-zo, shee mai kin,
ai ken gedda zeyzo. Pooral gal! Shee gadabi maidi poorli da
booddum-av. Eebin flaiunhai in da lidda, good vurr bootch gee-
bun voot warm. Ai habun nuvelt-inzwabba da bootch, avemar
voot shorder ntinner dan aldest shooibutt. Dat er nemun a dem,
al-baiumbai. Agamei! Wee tree dey davwa-rud vum da Gader-
all; zo da Zaiuns dellun. Leddun lib agina wail biu da waitishain
Nortar in im lajhum lungtaium.

Eldest now-sure (yes, indeed?) dying this time: she gave me her boots.
Costly boots! They two are from the No-Go-Zone of the North Lake
(clan? -land?). All Goddess's children have them some kind of No-Go-
Zone, now-by-and-by (now and forever). This one (Eldest) is all the way

65

from the Otterwaters, yes, m'lady! Them (expletive) traders never tell a person exactly where they get them; yes, but plenty of folk(s) know about otterseal fur. She is an ornery old motherdog most of the time; not giveaway nothing so long as life and breath still in (her) body. Yes, whatever, she is my kinswoman, I get to say so (if I choose). Poor old gal! She must be mighty poorly to put them off. Even (while riding?) in the litter, good fur boots would keep her feet warm. I have new-felted the interior of the boots, for my feet are smaller and thinner than Eldest's shoe-boats. That is what she called them, always. Alas! (I weep for her.) We are three days travois-road from the Gathering; so the signs say. May she live so long and see the pale NorthStar in his native home at last.

Aieee! Whichever nameless scholar it was, some five hundred solar years ago, who made the gloss on the Compiled Chronicles of the Polarization and added capitals and punctuation marks to the run-on text of this particular Chron, ten thousand blessings be upon her! Not everyone obliged by the times to pore over this ancient tome is an eager and willing scholar who delights in the drorish task of untangling the thoughts of yesteryear. Nor, for that matter, are some of us any kind of scholar. I, for instance, am a political prisoner, set to this task in lieu of harder work in the fields simply because I can read.[1] I can write, too, after a fashion; I am told that my strokestyle is nothing to write home about. Ha!

By thus dissembling, I am freed from the endless toil and bent backs of the poor copyists. I merely scritch out rough notes for a first-draft translation or to proof-confirm another's first draft. I work slowly but am reliably thorough and accurate, as dullards often are. My formal script is execrable and my composition childish at best.

DEER MOTHER: I AM WELLE I HAVE PLENTI EAT AND THEY TREET WE MERY WELLE?/.

---

[1]Ormunlatsans were known to hold all fragments of writing in great reverence, regardless of the burdensome task of translation. It is speculated that a mix of religious awe and possible leads to profitable treasure troves accounts for their putting hostage labor to that task. It lessened the weary workload of their own scribes and scholars.

I suppose I ought to be grateful; unlike my fellows of the field, I have a better than even chance of surviving my term of "service." But there are many times during the day that I look out on the sweating toilers to wish that I too could be handling the sturdy hoe instead of this delicate, beautiful, and all-too-fragile glass pen. My rations are meager enough as it is; they dock me food when I break a finely made "gahstling" nib. But I have managed to secure two or three turkey quills to write to you between the lines. In a pinch, I can use one of my long scholar's fingernails, properly cut to serve the purpose.

I AM DOING SCHOOLLAR COPY. O NO!! MY WURST SUJECT AT HOME. YOU WIL LAFH ME AT. PROUD ME OF WEN GOME HOME.

Oh, my mother!
I write to you in milk
that vanishes on the page.
As you fed me long ago
from flowing breast,
now I feed you intimate
knowledge of our enemy
that you may grow
in enmity against them
even as my own breast burns
with the giving.
Set slow careful flames
of controlled hate
to this page, dear mother!
Read in warm brown
what I set down
in wan, white,
snow-cold characters.

They have at least five thousand mares, half of that number ready to foal this autumn. They will be needing a great deal of fodder. Unless you can block the pass, flood the valley roads early, or complete the troop transport bypass canal before this winter, it will be best to send a guerrilla strike force to burn their hayfields by Midsummer's at the latest. The droughts come earlier here by a month or more, and if you bring some Greek fire, the June winds will whip up a firestorm they cannot put out. They will then have to import hay from Shangdo Province and you can attack their wains at several points along the route. Of course, they may make us Pollies do the firefighting; but lives must be risked in war.

Unfortunately, I am situated nowhere near the kitchens so I cannot employ subtle poisons as I did against the Tui-nah last mission. My ugly, unmar-riageable face, ungainly body and lame, shambling gait make them think me subnormal. They suppose me to be greedy also and desirous of more food, so they keep me underfed merely to feed their own gutswollen sense of self-importance. Little do they know that we who lodged with the nuns fasted as a rule. It sharpens our wits as it refines our perceptions. When I beg for milk, they give me the sour, whiskey-drugged dregs; I feed it to the stable guard dogs and get my own fresh mare's milk in the dark hours. The dogs are well-rested.

> Writing with milk
> in the moonlight
> white on white on white.
> Honor bright!

No one solicits me for bed-favors because I stink. I eat raw garlic every chance I get and rub pig dung on my outer clothing as a "religious" practice. The pages I work with also stink of dung (and not milk!). The other scholars insist that I work apart and, preferably, sleep in the barn. This suits me well for my nocturnal outings. Somehow my lameness disappears by night, along with my cumbersome scholar's garb. In tunic and silhouette, who goes there? Just another Ranger on night patrol.

> Swift as deerhound,
> owl in flight:

silent wingèd
cuts through night.

Defining my status as a political prisoner/family hostage was a brilliant stroke, dearest Ma! Under diplomatic rules, they cannot put me in chains (always a nuisance to pick open and relock); nor can they cage me.

As an honor-bound, they can, by rights, only insult and spit to try to make me run away or fight; my dull feeble-mindedness deflects their enmity: I bore them by my uncomprehending stare. I have not yet been obliged to punch one of them silly to put the Fear of the Exasperated Lamb into their weak hollow hearts. They curse you for sending them an obviously defective child—worthless as a hostage—and judge that you have cheated them of their rights to a properly valuable captive. They seem to give you respect for having cheated them. They are a most odd people, dear Mother.

The mares are foaling too early. One after the other, they are dropping horrid-smelling, ill-formed abortions. Scarcely one in two hundred carries her infant to term. Often, the mother bleeds to death as well. No wonder they are horse thieves! Their own stallions are anemic, short-winded and colicky.

P.S., Triday.

So are the women. I have been to the village. The glassworks is there, fueled by charcoal gathered from an obvious No-Go-Zone. Trees, small game, coydogs, all life thriving except our own kind.

Two more weeks later.

The women's work with the glass is remarkable to see: such deft grace carried out by such coarse hands. The glass pens are the chief trade item for them; the men take the pens and trade them for weapons and horses; the women get nothing, not even glory.

牧 曼 [Early summer][2]—Near haying time.

The warrior men, priests, and scholars, preening themselves on their superior status, insist that the broodwomen live closest to the No-Go-Zone. There is much amiss among the women and children. Perpetual sores and weak lungs are the best one can expect. Many children have badly bowed legs; the men crow over these saying they are born to be good riders. Few live long enough to prove the vain prophecies. Could you see them, Mother, you would pity our enemy as I have learned to do.

Many of them are not of this clan at all; they were made captive when pregnant and will not leave their first, beloved child. Then they are weakened by poor food and Zoneblood sickness. Many die by their own hand when their child dies.

How have these foes grown so numerous? It seems that high-status males take away their male infants at once from the birthing hut and give them to wet nurses who live near the men's quarters and act as sex workers when not nursing. No boy is a man until he has captured a smaller girl and kept her until he can impregnate her. If she is barren—or he is—she becomes a slave. Thus they breed up raiding armies perpetually at war. Broodwomen and slaves work the fields under the lash and in fear of being trampled or quartered by horses if they are caught fleeing.

真 寒 [Midwinter]

Alas for men's pride! And my own future. The prevailing winds have shifted. Something besides the blue spore and the phosphor ash is blowing through the men's camps.

---

[2]At this point, sealring timestamps begin appearing before the postscripts as the time between them increases (translations given, bracketed). These were drawn from the character set of pre-Polarization West-coastal Japanese characters, which became standardized during the Drift Invasion when refugees arrived in great numbers by floating cargo containers.

There is grave-sickness here. If you do not come soon, you need not come at all. Our foes will be dead by the hand of the Goddess alone.

𐤀 𐤁 [Spring equinox]

I do not know how to deliver this message to you without danger of infecting our people.

𐤀 𐤁 [Mid-spring]

If I can, I will dare to mount the hill by daylight and raise the Bone flag to ward you off. Soon, none will be left to guard the signal houses. I put the poison mark on the sheath of this missive as a warning.

Done! I have raised the flag. Few saw me, none opposed me. I added my own mark so you will know it was my deed. May the scouts see it in good time and not come too near! I have set those who recover to cry "Ware plague!" all along the borders.

Why do they obey me? There are none left to take charge of them; they follow me like sheep. There is plenty store of food but we eat sparingly lest the grain be the source of death. Only stores two or more years old are opened for rationing. We have no wild meat; only men hunt the deer and the bicattle. The pigs seem unaffected. Horse meat is taboo.

The plague ran like fire through the warriors and nurseries.[3] Only non-brood women and old men are left in any numbers. By the Goddess, I too

---

[3]A mark at the beginning of this note, presumed to be a timestamp, was blurred. The corner of the sheet was also attacked by mice while the pages were stored in a non-mercury-infused box. Based on the less darkly developed hue of the notes, some scholars hold that the Milk Texts from this point on were written in the year after the plague; this view is still considered controversial.

have been spared. Perhaps, as the old science says, small exposures, many times repeated, have proven my blood against the unknown germ-seed. I never bled the broodmares while they were in milk. I only mixed in the blood from healthy unmated mares. Perhaps Iaiana of the Ice Arrows and Deer Moon defended me from the disorder that struck down so many of our foes.

Perhaps the firewaters men mix with their kvass are tainted or their blood is pale. Their death-sweat is brown like brewed tealeaf.

I am tending the sick as best I can. Most of my fellow prisoners are ill. Our foemen die by the grain-measure every day. The enemy women help me to carry the bodies away. We cannot bury them and dare not burn them lest we send the sickness towards others downwind. We heap them in the fields and cover them with their belongings, then sacrifice a horse over the corpses. This is their religion, but it also seems the only sensible way to prevent the vultures from spreading the plague. Gorged on horsemeat, the birds leave human flesh to putrefy untouched.

Beloved Mother, I dare not return to the land and loins whence I came. I have seen too much of death, my Mother. Thousands upon thousands are dead—men, bicattle, and elkenherds alike. The herds die where they stand in untended grain fields and poison the hay. We have set the horses free to find their own pasturage. The barns are empty and the rats multiply. The smell of death is everywhere.

War is no longer the dearest object of my heart. Perhaps the Goddess hath willed it so.

I am leaving this place. I break faith and honor, but there are too few left to do more than disparage my name. All the chieftains are gone. None but small bands remain, too weak to war against you. The dead take no account of my faithlessness and dishonorable conduct.

⚕ ⚕ ☉ ⚔ [Heliacal rising of Blue—i.e., "BrightBlue," or Sirius]

I am leading the women and children away from here, as many as will follow me. Few enough! None of those who make the glass will come. I go towards the territories of our other great foe. If the sickness fells me later rather than sooner, they may suffer the same fate.

This is all I can do to assuage the just wrath of Du-Belicora, our War-Daimon. But I hope I do not reach them. What time I have left, I would rather devote to fostering these forlorn and broken former foes. Would that I could see your face, blessed Mother! After all these years of spurning motherhood myself, shedding the wise blood every moon as devotee to Du-Beli—what look would you wear to see me giving the LifeLaws to a pack of mongrel brats?

Farewell to my sisters of the blood, earth, and hearth. May you thrive and be as many as the stars in lasting love.

Notes found inside a pitch-sealed jar in a dry sandstone cave on the edge of the Nuvomeico Desert. Extended exposure to heat had brought out the secret milk-ink writing.

☉

In the decades since the discovery of these fragments, which were at first thought to be of little importance, patient scholarship has revealed a fuller picture of their context and significance.

These documents were written in the "female thread" altered characters, long thought to be merely decorative designs used by women to imitate the "look and feel" of revered (chiefly male) scholarly writings. They were, in fact, a secret cipher with poetry-derived keycode features used by a single lianbao-dang of the widely intermarried and geographically scattered Sangfra-Nwaling clan alliance.

Remarkably, the character set remained almost unchanged for more than thirty generations; thus, these desert-preserved documents are still legible to certain scholars today. They shed a new light on the mystery of the sudden demise of the once powerful Ormunlatsans who formerly occupied the high deserts of Rocquiyanl-Stonia.

It is now surmised that a variant of cow-stagger web-brain disease carried off the high-status meat eaters, leaving the milk and grain eaters relatively un-harmed, but dwindling within a generation or two as their offspring succumbed to the next waves.

The most thrilling aspect of the discovery is the passage that translates into code-talk the far older written record that predated the Polarization. With the hints and leadings provided by this translation it becomes possible to begin the work of translating at least one hundred similar pages among the many thousands of Ormunlat Temple fragments and other arcana held in scholarly hands worldwide. Scholars everywhere are eagerly converging upon the Cadian regions like fireants invading a root garden, hoping to carry off some succulent prize of new knowledge in fragments bigger than their their own heads can contain.

The importance of the findings persuaded the bao-dang's current generation to throw open their private means of communication in exchange for lasting worldwide prestige. Out of respect, publication was delayed until the death of the last clan Elder who was opposed to the disclosure and the revelation of the code's existence.

Violet Bertelsen

When the Circus
Came to Town

M ARIE SWUNG IN her hammock in the ship's hull, the heat of April so intense that she felt that she could reach out and touch it. As she swung back and forth, sweat dripping all over, a faint breeze came in through the portholes, and Marie took a deep breath and entered the panorama of her mind's eye. In her imagination, she prayed to the statue Eros, the winged perpetual youth with his bow and quiver, in the little shrine she kept inside her trunk, by her roots and oils. As sweat dripped on down, Marie saw the gold, wing-giving presence of Eros pour over her like grace; the imaginary candlelight filled the space, and Marie lost track of the who, the when, and the where as a great tide of ecstasy swept through her being.

And then, like a string pulled from her left temple to her solar plexus, Marie heard a voice in her heart say, "Go onto the deck." So she roused, damp and now cold in her grimy slip, fixed her hair with a band, and donned her dark, moon-and-star-spangled cloak, then stepped up the creaking ladder and made directly for Jessie, the pyrotechnic.

Jessie sat there in the kitchen on deck under the tarpaulin, feeding sticks to the rocket stove. A fish gumbo was cooking; members of the troupe lounged about the deck chatting, playing cards, and sleeping under the last light of dusk. Marie walked up, feeling sticky, outside of herself, and torpid. "What are you doing, Jessie?" she asked with a yawn.

Jessie smiled, his eyes flashing mischievously. "Cup of whiskey?"

Marie nodded. "Thank you kindly."

Jessie poured her a cup. "Caught a whole mess of fish in the shoal and I'm cooking them for the troupe. Some old-time river gumbo."

Marie took the cup of whiskey and squatted next to Jessie, trying to get back into her body fully. The invisible string pulled again, right by her solar plexus, and Marie looked down and picked up a stick. She examined it in the fading light. "This is elder wood, Jessie."

Jessie nodded, his smile fading. "What do you mean?"

"Burning elder summons evil spirits," said Marie, her face pinched and a cold sweat on her brow.

Jessie frowned. "I didn't mean anything by it."

"It's okay, Jessie, I'll burn some protective herbs and that should take care of the problem." Marie climbed down the creaking ladder into the hull, and opened her trunk to get the the last of her frankincense and bay leaves. She went back up, the little bags held in her teeth, then opened the bags, prayed over them, and threw them on the fire and fell to her knees, praying with all of her heart to Eros. She felt his rays of gold come through her hands like sunlight on water under a bridge. Then she sat down and picked up the cup of whiskey and took a long drink. "I hope that's enough."

Jessie laughed nervously, his eyes wide. "Me too. Last thing we need is an evil spirit."

"We should be fine," said Marie, the beads of sweat glistening with firelight all over her body, and she changed the subject as Jessie poured her another cup of whiskey. A few minutes later Jessie blew the conch shell to signal dinner, and the circus troupe roused themselves to the deck, tin cups and plates in hand.

A few hours later, Marie stumbled down the creaking stairs into the hull, drunk numb, her head spinning with the laughter and music that still roared around the kitchen on deck. She got into her hammock and fell promptly into a feverish sleep replete with dreams of leering demons, faces interwoven like spider webs, all throughout the ship's hull. Marie saw them swarm, and she fought them with pentagrams and holy names, but they slithered on by, all of them now concentrating on a point in the hull where they found a structural weakness. . . .

Right then screaming woke her. In the dark she heard rushing water as folks hollered and someone lit a lantern. The Ringleader screamed, with his full yell, "EVERYONE TO THE DECK!" Marie, still hungover, dreamy, and anxious, clumsily leapt from her hammock, tripping and falling into the foot-deep water, barely avoiding hitting her head on the trunk, and for a confused moment felt others rush past her, step on her as they ran towards the ladder. She felt herself begin to hover above her body, and thought, "So soon, Eros, my love?"

But Gabby grabbed her hand and hefted her up, and they clambered for the stairs as the water rose and the ship began listing more and more towards a disastrous angle.

A few minutes later the Ringleader and Mac came to the deck, faces red, clothing soaked, wet cigars clenched in their teeth. "We need everyone bailing water immediately!" the Ringleader commanded, and Mac began yelling instructions to the boatswain. Marie fell into place as buckets began passing down a line, from those down belowdecks, to the the trapeze artists and acrobats standing on the ladder and handing them up through the hatch, and then across the deck. Marie stood on the deck receiving the last bucket, emptying it into the river, and handing it to the clowns, who ran it back down down again. For what seemed like hours they worked in a nervous hush, bailing water as the boat crept south, its list slowly rectifying—until suddenly, a loud crash inside the hull accompanied by splashing and screaming ended the work.

As her shipmates swarmed around the hatchway, Marie stood nervously in place resisting the urge to crowd the scene, still holding the bucket. She found half of a cigarette in the pocket of her dress along with three matches, all mysteriously dry. She smoked her cigarette and waited, watching as the gray light of earliest dawn gathered. As the crowd at the hatchway scattered around the deck and their talk reached her, the story became all too clear. The stairs holding the three acrobats had broken. Sheila, who had been on the lowest rung, had gotten knocked out and drowned in the confusion. Michael, who'd been above her, had a serious wound to his leg where the splintered wood had bitten. Henry, right by the top, had managed to land without a scratch. The water sloshing inside the hull was now filled with blood. By the light of dawn Marie saw Mac limp the ship into some seedy docks. The Ringleader's face was white as a paraffin candle and Marie felt sick.

"Listen, everyone!" the Ringleader yelled, his face now red and voice projecting. "Marie, Jessie, and Doc, stay on board and tend the hurt. Mac, you and the strongmen work on the hull; Tom, Felipe, and Sue, come with me."

Michael's leg bled profusely. Marie guessed that the wood had stabbed right into his femoral artery. His face was white; he mumbled something, but Marie couldn't understand a single word. Doc gave him a shot of cayenne brandy and bound his wound with yarrow and calendula honey, and the blood stopped gushing, but Michael's color didn't improve, and he seemed insensible. Jessie managed to heft Sheila's body to the deck using an improvised rope ladder. Her face blue, a gash on the right side of her head, her eyes empty.

"I hope we can give her a proper burial," said Marie. "We can't keep her onboard for long in this weather." Already the morning was sticky with heat.

Doc tended Michael, feeding him nettle tea and checking his pulse, shaking his head. Marie knew already that he would die soon, too. She resolved her heart to be flinty and strong, but still, she felt tears pour down her face.

☉

The main tent had been sloshed with the bloody water, and so Mac and Denis took out the blue-and-orange-striped big top to clean in the sun. While they scrubbed it, they saw a group of children watching from the bushes near the bank.

"Hello!" hollered Mac, as the kids squawked and vanished into the underbrush like wild animals.

"Guess they know we're here," said Denis morosely as he dumped another bucket full of pink water into the beach.

By sundown the crew had managed to get almost all of the water out of the ship and Marie had made made a strong pine tea to clean the hull as best she could. Mac and Denis had made a new and stronger ladder, which Marie used to get down with the mop and five-gallon bucket half-full of strong pine tea. Once down below the deck she lit a lantern, and all at once found herself trembling with fear. "Dammit, Marie, pull yourself together," she said, and then began to cry. Michael, a long time ago, had been her lover. Sheila had always been a friend to everyone. She sobbed. "Pull yourself together!" she repeated, and then went to her trunk.

She opened it, grateful to see that no bloody water had entered. Marie pulled out the Rise to the Occasion condition oil she'd made last year, a little bottle of oil that had in it five-finger grass, mint, lemongrass, yarrow blossoms, bay leaves, a High John the Conqueror root, and a Solomon's seal root. She stripped naked, then took the oil and put a few drops on her hands. Starting at her feet, she anointed upwards, to the crown of her head. Then, in the mirror glued to the inside of the lid of the chest, she looked herself dead in the eyes and said, "I rise to the occasion! I rise to the occasion! I rise to the occasion!"

She exhaled, and said, "You just said it three times, Marie, now it's true." Then she put a little of the condition oil into the reservoir of the lamp, put her clothing back on, and mopped the hull with the pine tea, both the floor and the walls. While doing so, she focused all her intention on bringing cleansing, blessing and purification to bear. The heat caused her slip to become sticky with sweat in a matter of minutes. Soon the hull smelled like the middle of a forest.

Mac shouted down to Marie, "Come up, dear, we've made some dinner." She climbed up the ladder and then went down another to the shore, where Michael languished, his face deathly pale, and Doc and Jessie were helping themselves to the meal.

They sat around the fire in the midday heat, tossing green pine boughs on the coals to keep the mosquitoes away and eating a dismal meal of shriveled carrots, dried onions, and salt pork.

Afterwards they sat in tense silence. The fire crackled and mosquitoes attacked, and after a little while Marie took her hammock and strung it up between some trees, put the mosquito netting overhead, and lay down, praying inwardly, as Eros, the giver of wings, came to her and filled her with his golden light. She lost the thread, after some time, and drifted off to sleep.

Loud voices woke her in a panic.

"We got lost," boomed the Ringleader, "coming home in the dark. We're only few miles from Louisville, by a small agricultural community called Utica. Tomorrow we perform here."

"What will we do with Sheila's body?" asked Mac. "It's already beginning to stink in the heat."

"Do we have enough wood to burn her?"

Mac shook his head. "No sir, not now."

The Ringleader shrugged. "We'll have to wait until after tomorrow." Marie heard him directing some men to take Sheila's body away in a hammock and to tie her in a tree so the coyotes couldn't get her. She shivered and fell back asleep.

That morning the circus troupe loaded the tent, ropes, and ties to a cart, and Mac hitched Benny the mule to carry the load into town. The Ringleader set forth and the performers all began walking into town.

Arnie, one of the clowns, walked on his hands by Marie. "The Ringleader says it's about five miles to town," he said.

Marie shrugged and kept on walking. "Long enough to take a roll in the bushes and still catch up," Arnie elaborated. He panted like a dog with his tongue out and then flipped back on to his feet in one fluid motion.

Marie raised an eyebrow. "Arnie, I can't simply forget the time you called me a 'disgusting shemale' in front of everyone."

Arnie winked. "Any port in a storm."

Gabby, the fire-breather and sword-swallower, shot Arnie a look that meant trouble. "Okay, buster, leave it off before I tickle your ribs."

Arnie laughed again. "Always trust it to the fire-breathers to give you a hard time," he said, and then ran ahead to say something to Denis.

Gabby shook her head. "One of these days I swear I'm going to slap that man!"

"Well, please not on my account!"

They walked in a cold, tense silence, Gabby rubbed her hands on her elbows, as if something were eating at her. "What are we going to do about the tent after Sheila died right near it?" asked Gabby, eyes wide.

"We washed it in the river and set it out in the sun. You can't see the blood, and nothing purifies like sunlight."

Gabby shook her head. "I don't like it, I don't like it one little bit. What more can we do?"

"Well, I mopped inside the hull with pine tea, but I'm all out of herbs after purifying the fire where Jessie was burning elder wood. If I could smoke out the inside of the tent that would help."

"I swear, if he weren't the Ringleader's son.... Anyways, we'll get some herbs and won't have to touch a single silver penny."

When they reached town, Marie and Gabby left the troupe and went off to the general store. Inside, a pasty-faced man sat over a food-stained newspaper, smoking hashish. The energy of the place felt to Marie sticky, polluted, and spoilt like bad milk. The man looked up myopically.

"How can I help you ladies?" he creaked.

"We need some bay leaves," said Marie.

The shopkeep stared at both of them. "Never seen you around before, where you from."

"The circus—we're headed to Louisville," said Gabby.

"Why you wearing a dress, boy?" he asked Marie.

"I'm a fortune teller," she replied.

The shopkeep shrugged and took a big hit off his pipe. "We don't got no bay leaves here," he said, smoke drifting out of his mouth.

"Do you got angelica?"

"No."

"Rosemary?"

"No. This is a small town where people grow their own herbs, you understand."

"Do you have *any* herbs?"

The shopkeep hefted himself up and looked about. "We got an old bag of myrrh—old doctor used to use it for wounds and teeth, but he died three years ago. Ain't no one wanted it since. I'd sell it to y'all for two silver pennies. Then there's some salt and pepper." He sat down again.

"We'll take the myrrh? And a bottle of wine."

"Four silver pennies," replied the clerk, getting up and retrieving the paper bag of myrrh, then handing them a jug of table wine.

"If you make it zero you and your family can see the circus for free," suggested Gabby, taking four tickets from her brassiere.

The clerk considered that, put a piece of hashish in his pipe, and held it to a candle. "You got yourself a deal."

They slipped out of the store and found the rest of the troupe raising the tent. When they had it up, Marie built a fire inside of pinewood, and let the fire die down to coals. Over the coals she threw the pound of myrrh, slowly, praying over it that the evil would stop right there. She performed a banishing ritual, tracing the arcane shapes in the dense haze of smoke, vibrating the Names and filling the space with dazzling astral light. Then she threw in the last of the myrrh. The inside of the tent was milky with the thick, fragrant smoke. Her eyes burned and she prayed as the last of the myrrh burnt, and then she poured the wine on the coals as an offering to wing-giving Eros. The embers died, and then Marie slipped out of the tent to prepare for the show.

Old Marge got her little tent ready to sell the tickets and Mac fired up the oven to roast ears of corn and hotdogs. A line began to form outside. Inside the tent, the Ringleader walked around giving everyone the signal, and then the evening began. Marie watched from backstage, in the place she always did, praying silently that everything would go well.

The Ringleader began to shout his opening lines, and the crowd hushed. "Ladies and gentleman, boys and girls, welcome to the circus—where a marvelous, magical time will be had by all!" he bellowed. And Doc began to blare on his trumpet, Ellie on the xylophone, Jessie on the drums, and Xave on the accordion; the audience watched with glee as the clowns did their slapstick routine, getting in the way of the Ringleader who then chased them away by cracking his bull whip in the air. With the crack, the music stopped, except for a drum roll.

"And now to introduce our marvelous magical acrobats, who will make one and together a huuuuuuman pretzel!" The two strongmen came in carrying the five acrobats on their backs on huge platters. The strongmen lifted the acrobats over their heads and they leapt from platter to platter and formed human pyramids, and inverse human pyramids, then contorted themselves wildly, feet over head; a big man fit into a tiny box, trapeze artists caught each other while swinging in the air, all to raucous ragtime music.

Marie felt the soar of the music commingled with the energies of the performers stretch and tighten till it pulled taut like ten thousand parallel strings and then, in an instant, it released and the crowd lost their minds, screaming, hollering, and applauding wildly. Out came the clowns, dressed in drag like strippers from the old world, big fake blond wigs, tight fishnet stockings and little miniskirts; they danced around the audience soliciting money and the crowd threw popcorn at them.

Next came the jugglers, who, faster and faster, juggled many and increasingly dangerous objects. Swords sharp enough to slice paper began to fly through the air, Gabby blindfolded between the whizzing blades. When the band struck a note, David cut Gabby's bound hands and she undid her hoodwink, took his sword, and with utmost dramatic flair, swallowed it. Marie saw the strings of light grow taut again, and then Gabby pulled out the sword and swung it out over her head triumphantly; the band started playing an old jazz standard, syncopated, with a deep groove, and the crowd exploded in applause, screaming as one.

Gabby began to blow fire, and behind her came two dancers, swinging balls of fire on chains through the air with grace, as the groove deepened. And then came a tinkling piano melody in parody of the previous song, and out came the clowns again, juggling felt swords, comically stabbing each other through, falling over in heaps and pretending to die until all were on the ground. The tightrope walker strutted over the audience's head sixty feet above, and the strongmen tied steel rods into overhand knots. Finally the whole troupe gathered in a great circle around the inside of the tent and danced madly to a klezmer song, until at last the music ended, the performers threw up their hands, and Marie put her fingers in her ears to muffle the deafening roar of the audience.

The Ringleader came out in his frock coat, top hat in hand, and took a bow. "And that, ladies and gentlemen, boys and girls, concludes our show—but not the circus! We have the finest whiskey from the great stills of Pittsburgh to buy at the little cantina, hot dogs galore, and Sybil the transvestite oracle will consult her cards to read your future. Stay around and try your hand at our many games of skill and chance with which to attract your fancy."

Marie roused herself from her prayers and set up a little table by the side of the tent and then lit a small lantern to cast a circle of light on her tarot cards. She looked over the table in her turban adorned with cut glass and ostrich feather at the small trickle of people filing out of the tent. Many stopped to mill about, others purchased whiskey, popcorn, or sausages on bread.

Momentarily, a tall, good-looking man with a blond handlebar moustache and gentle blue eyes came and sat down. Marie smiled at him, her guard down.

"I wish that I may consult the oracle," he said.

"Who may need to know the future?" she asked

"Argeniz Davidson."

"What may Mr. Davidson wish to know?"

Argeniz shifted in his chair, his eyes looking downward at the table, and then at Marie. "This is hard to make into a single question. Here's the situation: the Sheperdsons and the Grangerfords are two old families here that have been rivals for longer than anyone can remember. It probably started with cattle rustling, but no one can remember. For many years, the police force restrained violence from spiraling out of control. Most of the folks around here are farming families, you see, and scratch out a living farming, gardening and selling livestock to Louisville. And for a while most people could remain neutral, but in the past few months everything has heated up—last week three houses got burned, and five people were shot dead. Usually this represents more violence than we see in a year. Basically, I want to know how will this situation turn out."

"What is your role in all of this?"

"I'm the country sheriff, elected to stay impartial in a town where, increasingly, impartiality gets one a few ounces of hot lead."

Marie shuffled the cards and cut them, blessed them, and dealt them on the table. She looked at them a good long time.

"The Eight of Swords," she began. "You are in a situation you do not fully understand and must navigate by feelings. The King of Swords reversed … What I see here, Mr. Davidson, is that there are forces also that are trying to keep you in the dark, and to undermine your efforts. You cannot trust those you think you can; you have already been betrayed, although the exact manner of this remains unknown to you now. Now, see the Seven of Swords: that means that dishonesty abounds. And the Seven of Cups is opposite—you are stretched thin by a bunch of competing options you don't know how to appraise. Below the situation is the Devil—folks have become the willing slaves of a monstrous situation—and above, Death: this will end with no way back to the way things were before. The Page of Swords reversed represents the people around, and that means that they are small-minded, drunk with their petty power, and constantly undermining you. Justice, here, represents your hopes and dreams—you wish to remain balanced, just and fair. And the final card is the Six of Swords." She looked up at him. "Soon, Sheriff, you will leave this town by boat, and may or may not return."

Sheriff Davidson considered the cards for moment, and then took a few notes in the same small notebook he used to take notes for his police work.

"Thank you," he said, blowing air out of his lungs slowly like a tea kettle. "That does sum the situation remarkably well."

"Should you like another reading, sheriff?" asked Marie.

"No, ma'am, that was enough to consider for a long time. How much do I owe you?"

"A silver penny, please."

Sheriff Davidson gave Marie a penny, and as she put it in the little box under the table, he gave her another one. "For you," he said with a disarming smile.

Marie bowed her head. "Thank you, sir."

He put on his straw hat and ambled off, and behind him was a long line of others wanting to know the future that the cards would reveal. The circus continued merrily until well after dawn, when the last customers finally stumbled drunkenly home.

The circus folk loaded up the cart, Benny the mule got hitched up, and Mac led him back towards the boat, the troupe following, carrying supplies, weary and exultant. When they got to camp, though, the euphoria quickly dissolved as a large wake of vultures flapped away and they caught the deep stench of Sheila's and Michael's now bloated corpses filling the air.

Marie raised her voice, face red, fists clenched. "We cannot let their bodies rot here like this," she screamed. "The dead don't stay restful when they come to a bad end."

The Ringleader nodded slowly, and began yelling in his enormous voice, pointing, ordering strongmen to gather wood, and the rest to build a funeral pyre. The Ringleader delegated the lighting of the pyre to his son Jessie, tasked Doc with reading something appropriate from the Bible before the fires started, and then quietly told Marie to come with him into the boat.

They climbed the ladder to the deck and then the new ladder down into the hull, which smelled antiseptically of pine resin. Marie rolled a cigarette from her little pouch, struck a match to light it, and began smoking it nervously.

"What's the situation here," asked the Ringleader in a low tone, "the real situation?"

"Bad, seriously bad," Marie answered. "Looks like the town has two factions that are at each other's throats in some sort of formless, escalating vigilante warfare. Increasingly other people are getting swept along in the rising tide of bloodshed, and no one can remain neutral for long. My thought is that we need to get out of here as fast as possible."

The Ringleader considered that for a moment, then lit a cigar and began to smoke it and pace. "I'll get everyone working on the ship as soon as possible, and we can leave the day after tomorrow and do a show in Louisville—we got big crowds there last year."

They both stood there silently smoking, watching from the portholes as the pyres blazed, heavy smoke rising up into the sky under a hot sun the color of hammered gold. After a while, as the fires died down, they both returned to the little beach where Mac had made a big pot of soup, and was serving it with whiskey—"To commemorate," he intoned solemnly as he filled each person's little tin cup. There the troupe sat, silently eating and drinking, before everyone slunk away to find a patch of shade to sleep during the heat of the day.

Marie drowsed in the golden light of her inner world, unfocused, torpid from want of sleep, and soon dreamt of vicious dogs.

Screaming woke her, and she saw policemen yelling, strongmen's and clowns' arms folded as they listened, and the Ringleader with face red. The policemen had their hands on their holstered revolvers, and the Ringleader seemed to be trying to defuse the situation. A moment later the police led the Ringleader away.

With nothing to do about it and no direction, the entire circus troupe milled about angrily on the beach. Gabby saw Marie returning and explained, "They took our Ringleader—said we can't be just burning bodies, and he took the fall."

"That isn't going to end well...."

Doc shouted to try to get everyone to listen, but couldn't raise his voice loud enough. Mac tried to do the same, stuttering as he did when stressed, but no one paid him heed. Just then, Jessie lifted his voice into an unaccustomed boom, and the troupe became immediately silent. "Look, folks," he bellowed, "we need to figure out how to get the Ringleader back. The town doesn't care about a few dead carnies. What they care about is getting a bribe. We need to do two things: first we need to fix this boat; second we need to get the Ringleader back. Mac, what do we need to fix the boat?"

"A b-b-barrel of t-t-tar," stuttered Mac, his ashen face twitching terribly.

Jessie said, "Fine; some of us will go to town and buy tar and see about figuring out who to bribe. We'll buy food too. The rest of us will stay here and guard the camp."

That settled, Mac fed Benny and hitched the cart, and called Jessie, Marie, and Doc to come along. The road stretched on muddy and rutted. The little crew walked, grimly, without saying a word. When they arrived, Doc and Mac entered the general store to get food, and Marie and Jessie went looking for the Ringleader.

Jessie's mouth formed a hard thin line and Marie smoked a cigarette as they wandered around town, feeling the faces watching them through the curtains. They came upon a drunk man struggling to pull up his pants. "Where's the jail?" asked Jessie.

The man blanched as he fumbled with his belt. "Yonder ways," he said, gesturing with his head, "not a place I'd like to be, no sir, no sir." Jessie and Marie headed towards the center of town, following the drunkard's directions.

They walked in the full blaze of the heat of the day, feeling worn and drugged. By the crossroads near the general store was a man on horseback. Marie lifted her eyes. "Sheriff Argeniz Davidson, what luck!" she said with a smile. "Just the man I wished to see right now."

He turned and nodded with an unreadable expression. "How may I help you?"

"Our Ringleader was arrested—we wish to bail him out and get out of town."

The sheriff shifted in his saddle. "News to me, what's he held for?"

"Burning some bodies that perished in our shipwreck."

He shifted in his saddle again, frowning and considering. "I'll see what I can do," he said resolutely. "Obviously the bodies were yours and not anyone here, and you have your own circus laws that don't concern the town. There's no reason for us to hold your Ringleader."

"Thank you, sir," said Marie.

"I wouldn't suggest you two go anywhere the jail now. You two are not safe here."

Jessie nodded bitterly. "Got it," he said.

Argeniz cleared his throat. "If I may, ma'am, please meet me back here around dawn tomorrow. I have a favor to ask."

Marie nodded her assent, and without another word Argeniz turned and headed towards the jail. Marie and Jessie, after getting a bit lost in the sprawling, decayed strip of ancient suburb, managed to find Doc and Mac with a wagon loaded with flour, salt pork, and onions. They both looked distraught. "No tar in town," said Mac. "Might try looking for some pine pitch in the forests."

Marie shook her head with a sense of bitter foreboding like sediment on her tongue. "Not here, Mac. You'd get shot or worse if someone found you." They rode back to camp in anxious silence.

That night while the circus troupe had dinner as the light of day faded and the mosquitoes assumed their time of dominance, they heard distant popping noises coming from the direction of town.

"Wonder why they're watching fireworks?" asked Arnie the clown.

"Those aren't fireworks," said Jessie, his blue eyes blazing and his lips drawn in his sandy blond beard, "that's gunfire."

Little popping noises, faraway and faint, seemed so innocent, almost silly, but somewhere beyond the veil of twilight and insects, hot lead was sending people down into bloody heaps. Dinner over, Marie heard the noises continue into the night, then shivered in the hot sticky air and laid down in her hammock to sleep. She dreamt that night of Sheriff Argeniz. She woke before dawn and cast her cards for the day by the embers of the fire, took in what they told her, then bundled her things and began to walk into town alone.

In the gray, eerie light, Marie moved quickly, foxlike, along the five miles to town. Marie had learned many years ago to walk both quickly and invisibly, like a wild animal, to skulk silently in among shadows. About halfway to town she passed a big farmhouse surrounded by razorwire. Something about the property made her take pause. As she crouched in the grass, it seemed like a black smoke was rising, and there were some—odd trees or something—and then the shapes resolved and she saw that there were about six heads on pikes staring ghoulishly right out at her. Her heart ringing in her ears, she redoubled her will and continued slipping through the shadows towards town.

Reaching the crossroads by the general store, she waited some thirty minutes until she saw Sheriff Davidson, who approached her. "Morning," he said with his eyes glinting, his face gold in the gentle light of sunrise.

"Good morning," said Marie, still a bit shaken.

"What's wrong?"

"Walking here I saw a big farmhouse with six heads on pikes, right by the kitchen garden, like scarecrows."

Argeniz didn't say anything for a long moment, "Okay. Got it. Okay, there's a nice cafe round the corner, you hungry?"

Marie nodded and Argeniz led her to a cafe about half a mile from the general store, where they got a booth by the very back. The sheriff said, "I'll get whatever you want. On me."

"Thank you."

They looked at the menus and the sheriff got a big carafe of coffee, with a little pot of cream and bowl of sugar, and some bacon with eggs and hash browns. Marie ordered the potato omelet. The waitress got them the carafe of coffee along with two bone china cups with matching saucers, and disappeared.

"You know, Marie, I am not partisan," said the sheriff. "I simply want to maintain law and order. Law and order allows for certain things that everyone likes, like your circus."

Marie took a sip of the delicious brew. "I had a sense that things were bad here but I didn't let myself imagine that they were quite 'heads on pikes,' especially so close as you are to Louisville."

"The town fathers of Louisville don't want to stick their hands in this hornet's nest either; their attitude continues to be, 'Let the animals kill each other and then we'll turn the place over to military law and prison labor camps.'"

Marie shivered.

"This is why I felt it necessary to hire you."

The food arrived; the waitress placed it with a few jocular words and vanished while the two ate. A little later Argeniz pulled out a small leather bag with the clink and clang of silver. "Shall we?"

Marie cleared a spot on the table and got her cards. She laid aside the cloth they were wrapped in, shuffled the cards, blessed them, cut them, and then dealt them on the table.

Argeniz studied the cards and then looked at her face. "What do they mean?"

"They are very similar to the cards I pulled for you at the circus. The situation remains the same, although the actions that have opened for you are now quite different. The King of Pentacles has entered: there is someone that you can appeal to who will help you resolve your problems through generosity. Then, there, we see the Queen of Cups, so there may be a love interest. We see the Six of Swords again ... but now the final card is the Eight of Wands. Swiftness—things from now on are going to happen really fast."

Argeniz took careful notes on his police pad, asking Marie to repeat some of the details. He then sat for a long moment frowning. Finally he shook himself and said, "One more reading please—a love reading."

Marie smiled; she always enjoyed doing love readings. She shuffled the cards, blessed them, cut them, and pulled three: the Queen of Swords reversed, the Two of Cups, and the Fool. "It looks like you come from a nasty relationship with a severe and shrewish woman," she said. "You are currently in the process of falling in love—might be short-term, might be long-term, I can't tell—but we see with the Fool that this love will lead into adventures and experiences you cannot yet dream of."

Argeniz glanced at Marie's eyes for a moment. She caught a rosy blush on his cheeks and then he laughed a little, scribbled on his police pad, and said under his breath, "Wonderful, how wonderful."

Just then the front windows shattered, and whizzing noises filled the air. Argeniz grabbed Marie, pulled her down underneath the table, and whispered hoarsely: "They're shooting up the place—we need to leave immediately!"

They crawled to and through the kitchen, and at the back of it they got up and the sheriff led her down through the basement, with its endless mason jars on dusty shelves and melancholy sacks of potatoes and onions, to a door that opened up to daylight by a compost pile. They slipped through the shadows to a rundown brick building where Argeniz opened the heavy door with a key and entered.

"What happened?" whispered Marie.

"Some people just tried to murder us. Like I say, the greatest risk lies with those who don't take a side. This is my safehouse—no one but you and me and Tabitha, who you'll meet shortly, know about it. We're okay for the moment." Argeniz shook himself and then poured a small glass of brown liquid from an ornately cut bottle. "Brandy?"

"Please."

Argeniz paced around his safehouse, while Marie, in spite of herself and the situation, took an immediate like to the place. On the walls hung tasteful Renaissance prints—Dürer, Rubens, and Rembrandt. She noticed that the sheriff had several bookshelves crammed with books, and a then a tabby cat rubbed her face on Marie's legs, purring pleasantly.

Argeniz smiled and stopped pacing. "As I promised: Marie, meet Tabitha; Tabitha, meet Marie. Tabitha, I may add, is an excellent judge of character."

With a sigh he sat down in a chair, nursing his brandy and thinking quietly. In the near distance they heard popping of gunfire, and Marie's heart raced. A long time passed in silence before Marie asked in a whisper, "Do you have a plan?"

"Almost."

Argeniz studied his police pad a moment, and then his eyes brightened. "We leave tonight by moonlight for Louisville; I have some colleagues there who may be sympathetic to sending some officers to this town."

Marie look frightened. "But what of my circus?"

"They are still stuck, right?"

"The general store didn't have the supplies we need to make a patch."

"We'll go to Louisville and get the supplies you need to fix the boat. I can't leave you here to try to get back to them on your own. It's too dangerous. We'll wait here until darkness falls and then we go—a journey by water."

For a little while the two waited uncomfortably in a tense silence, not quite knowing what to do or say. Marie felt she was in way over her depth, and the day was till young, with hours left of sunlight. Argeniz paced around the house for a little while, before asking "Do you like stories, poetry?"

"I love them."

"I have many. We can read them to each other to make the time go by faster." He took a small volume bound in blue cloth and began to read one of Shakespeare's love sonnets. Not to be outdone, Marie found Pablo Neruda's love poetry on the shelf and read one in decent Spanish. For an hour they passed around sonnets, and then had lunch and resumed with Borges stories, and then an old yellowed sci-fi magazine, and then more poetry.

As they read, the sun cut more and more westerly, and soon dusk was falling. Argeniz gathered up a few guns and many rounds of ammunition and gave Marie a canteen, and they carried a paddle each. Above their heads they carried a small rowboat made of painted cork. They slipped out in the moonlight, taking a serpentine path through alleyways and back roads to a canal, which they rode surreptitiously to the Ohio river. And then they were on their way to Louisville under a waxing gibbous moon.

By moonlight they navigated the little craft down the river, and after a few minutes the crazed violence of Utica's fighting factions and the beached, cursed circus seemed to belong to a very different world.

"How did you learn to read?" asked Argeniz. "So few people do nowadays."

"My mom and dad taught me. They treasured the old learning traditions quite a bit—but then when the hemorrhagic fever came through when I was thirteen years old, they both died. For a few years I stayed with my aunt, who taught me how to read the cards, but she got to drinking and cursing and running with a bad crowd, so I had to leave one night when I was fifteen, promising myself that I'd only ever use magic for good. And I took my cards and painted my face and ran off to the river where I joined the circus." Marie grew silent now in the silver light of the moon.

Argeniz nodded. "My parents made sure that I had the reading and math skills that I'd need for a political life, and that involved reading a lot of old books; and once I started I couldn't stop—one book opened another, and I read all night, by the dim light of a candle in secret, nurturing my one solitary virtue: curiosity."

"A fitting virtue for solving crimes."

Argeniz nodded and gave Marie an unreadable look.

For a moment there was silence between them, and then Argeniz whispered, "Marie," and he touched her hair while looking into her eyes. She put her hand over his, and dropped her eyelids to receive his kiss. And with a gasp they rolled in the moonlight, kissing, and stroking; his strong hands felt over her body, pulling her towards him, touching her back and down her legs and then—

He stopped suddenly, a look of panic and fear on his face.

"I thought you knew," said Marie, voice small and frightened, heartbeat ringing in her ears.

Argeniz got his face on pinched and tight and rowed the boat mechanically towards the south. Marie sat in the prow and cried as silently as possible.

A few hours later they had arrived in Louisville. Argeniz and Marie both said nothing as they brought the boat to shore. Finally Argeniz cleared his throat: "I ... I'm not just going to abandon you here, Marie. First we go and talk with some of my colleagues here, and then we can get the tar for you to patch your ship."

Marie nodded, and Argeniz sighed. Once they were standing on the shore, Argeniz touched Marie's shoulder, and then to her surprise kissed her on the mouth. She brought her hands to his face. Argeniz laughed and restrained himself. "We have to either find a place to stash our boat or carry it with us and into the regional sheriff's office," he said.

"Let's carry it, I would hate to get stuck here."

So they walked through Louisville's thronging streets carrying the boat on their shoulders, carefully avoiding stepping into the filth of the gutters. After about ten blocks they reached the Sheriff's office.

"Come with me, Marie," said Argeniz, and they entered the brick building and leaned the boat and paddles against a wall. Inside were some portly policemen typing on typewriters and smoking cigarettes. "Argeniz!" said one with Nordic features and an air of nihilism. "So good to see you."

"Hello, Harry. I hope you don't mind that I brought my fortune teller."

"Not at all—please come in."

Argeniz and Marie sat down in chairs. "Things are bad in Utica," said Argeniz. "A few hours ago bullets intended for my head tore through the Early Bird Cafe."

Harry took a pack of cigarettes from his pocket and offered one each to Argeniz and Marie, and they sat there smoking for a moment.

"Look, Argeniz, I'll be blunt with you. We don't have the resources to do much for Utica at all. Our forces are spread pretty thin right now securing more valuable land to the south where gang warfare has been heating up. Utica is a little cow town. After the Grangerfords and Shepherdsons kill enough of each other off in a few years, we'll probably come through with the army, try whoever's left for murder, hang them to cheering crowds, and then carve up the land to give to retiring officers. That's just how we do here; you won't get military intervention for a few years at least, and until then, I'd strictly stay out if you want to save your hide." They all smoked in tense silence for a long moment.

"Look," said Argeniz finally, "I promised Marie here to help get her beached circus ship out. Do you know if there is a store close by that might sell some tar for patching a ship?"

Harry shook his head. "You're a fool, Argeniz—why are you messing around with circuses?"

Argeniz spoke with immense dignity, his face wreathed with smoke: "Sir, you know I'm only as good as my word."

Harry croaked out a laugh. "You crazy bastard. There's a shipwright supply shop a few blocks to the north, by the new canal. They got tar, sails, rigging, and anything else you care to name to save your circus, but look, I told you—get out, give me a call, we can find a place for you here. Look Argeniz, I'm just being real with you. In normal times we'd be able to send a few thousand men down to Utica, but we ain't in normal times."

Argeniz nodded. "Thank you. I understand," he said, and Harry shook hands with him and then Marie. Argeniz and Marie got their boat and walked two blocks to the north.

Argeniz paid for the tar, and as they lowered the boat into the canal and the tar barrel into the boat, then headed to the river, he wore a slack face. "So there goes my life work," he said, letting out his breath painfully. "Either I leave with my skin intact, or I stay and die."

Marie said nothing, but felt a tender string pull. She went over to Argeniz, touched his face, and then brought her lips to his. They began to kiss, and soon tethered the boat in a shady little cove, as the golden light of Eros descended over them and they made love. They fell asleep in each other's arms and slept until night fell and the moon rose.

Silently, by the light of the moon, they returned to to Utica, Marie exultant, sitting on the barrel of tar, Argeniz silent and lugubrious. After a few hours they stopped by the circus boat. Marie put her fingers in her mouth and whistled loudly four long blows; a return whistle came three times fast, and she whistled back two short notes. Then she saw the faces of Mac and Jessie come out from the darkness.

"We got tar," she said, "tar to fix the boat." Mac and Jessie got right to work building a fire, and began rousing others and getting everything in order to patch the boat.

Argeniz regarded Marie, and Marie touched his face and said, "Please return before we leave; it'll take hours before we can sail off."

Argeniz nodded and gave a kiss on her lips, and then slipped away.

Marie saw Gabby and hailed her. "Oh friend! I have the loveliest things to tell you!"

Gabby kissed Marie on the cheek in greeting without smiling, her face tense and strained. "And I the worst: the Ringleader is dead. He was hanged the other day with all the other prisoners."

Marie felt tears fall down her cheeks and felt suddenly exhausted and old. She slunk away to her hammock to sleep, her heart heavy with grief and foreboding.

About six hours later, the hole had been patched well enough to get going to Louisville, and the troupe began packing up morosely in the mid-morning heat. Jessie made the rounds, dispirited, not yet able to quite fill the shoes of his new role.

He saw Marie. "We leave in a few hours," he said, a tear in his voice. "Do you maybe have some herbs or something to help with my voice? I find it hard to yell loud enough."

Marie motioned, and they both went down into the hull. She opened her trunk and handed Jessie a root. "Here's some calamus root," she said. "It helps with the throat and helps with commanding others. It's what I gave your father."

Jessie breathed in sharply and began chewing the root, tears falling down his cheeks. Marie fumbled around her trunk and after a moment found what she was looking for—the Rise to the Occasion condition oil. She said to Jessie, "May I?" He nodded his assent, so she put some of the oil on her hands and prayed over it, and then, starting at Jessie's chin, she brought her hands upwards towards the crown of his head, anointing Jessie with the oil.

"You rise to the occasion!" she said, and Jessie nodded. Marie repeated, "You rise to the occasion!" Jessie nodded again, and Marie told him, "Say it."

Jessie mumbled, "I rise to the occasion?"

"Like you mean it!"

"I rise to the occasion."

"Scream it!"

"I rise to the occasion!"

Marie looked Jessie dead in the eyes. "You said it three times—now it's true."

Marie packed her things slowly, looking over her shoulder every thirty seconds or so to see if Argeniz would return. Night began to fall and still no sign of him.

Mac came to her. "We're leaving soon."

Marie felt numb and said softly, "But Sheriff Argeniz ..."

"We can't wait for him. C'mon, Marie, we got to get out of here while we still can."

Marie nodded, began to cry, and loaded her gear into the hull. When she finished, she stood on the deck looking for the Sheriff. The moon rose, and then she heard paddling, and saw the little boat lurching down the river. "Argeniz!"

she cried.

The strongmen and Arnie and Michael and Doc came over, and a few jumbled minutes later the sheriff and his little boat were on the deck. Argeniz was covered in soot, his clothing torn, a sad look on his face, and a yowling cat in his hands, "I returned to my safehouse to find it set on fire, and I barely got Tabitha out before they started shooting at me. So I slipped into my boat and got here ... and now everything I have in the world is with me on this deck."

Mac said, "Well, we can at least take you to Louisville."

Jessie looked at both Marie and Argeniz for a moment, cleared his throat, and said with confidence, "We could use someone skilled with guns on board, as security for the circus. Especially someone friendly with the law enforcement in this area. You could stay with us if you should like. We'll keep you fed and housed."

Argeniz nodded, hugged Marie closer to him and managed to smile, and then laugh. "Why not?" he said, "I've fallen in love with a fortune-telling transvestite, lost everything, and so yes, please, now's the time to join the circus."

Those on deck cheered, Doc came up with some whiskey and poured everyone a drink, a toast to love was made, and after some brief words, the exhausted carnies stumbled belowdecks and up into their hammocks while the crew directed the boat to Louisville beneath the full moon.

Contributors

Nathan Beebe Peltier (cover art) is a visual artist raised in Minnesota. He studied Geology at Northland College in Wisconsin, and Ecological Design and Architecture at ECOSA Institute in Arizona. Lake Superior and the high desert have informed him and his work. Nathan currently works primarily with ink and digital mediums, but has been known for tattooing, electroformed jewelry, and block printing. He is inspired by architecture, dreams, love, and the apocalypse.

Pierre Magdelaine was born in Paris, France, about thirty years back and has scarcely been away since. For a few years, however, he's been exploring the exciting new continent of the English language, telling stories about dichromat private eyes, paranoid structural engineers, adventurous shepherds and birds of all feathers. You can learn more and play a silly game (with birds) at https://pimagides.com/. ◊ Cave Avem.

Dawn Vogel edits reports for historians and archaeologists. In her alleged spare time, she runs a craft business, co-runs a small press, and tries to find time for writing. Her steampunk adventure series, *Brass and Glass*, is available from DefCon One Publishing. She is a member of Broad Universe, SFWA, and Codex Writers. She lives in Seattle with her husband, author Jeremy Zimmerman, and their herd of cats. Visit her at http://historythatneverwas.com.

Daniel Chawner lives in New Jersey with his wife and two children. He works as a Software Manager for a bank in New York City. While not writing or driving between soccer fields, Daniel enjoys biking, hiking, and watching the Mets try to play baseball. You can find more of his writing at chawner.net.

Jonathan Reif is based in Berlin, Germany, and does various odd jobs to keep himself and the Prussians amused. He was concerned about the energy crisis until discovery of Jevon's paradox, after which he was merely worried. When it comes to hot chips and variations thereof, the author prefers *patatas bravas*, the thinking man's French fries.

Jeff Burt lives in Santa Cruz County, California, and works in mental health. He has contributed to *Per Contra, Bird's Thumb, Gold Man Review, Lowestoft Chronicle*, and won the 2016 Consequence Magazine Fiction Prize.

David England lives the small-town life in eastern Wisconsin on the shores of Lake Michigan, along with his talented wife, Anne; her amazing artwork; and the many voices in his head telling him what he should be writing next.

G. Kay Bishop began last year with a big push to complete a 608K-word novel and ended it with a big chance to appear in *New Maps*. How lucky can some people get? On the other hand, the word "housework" strikes dread into the astral sphere of the autochthonous artist, deeply immured in the dark, hollow spaces of Other Worlds. Ya pays yer money and ya takes yer choice.

Violet Bertelsen grew up in the soft woodlands of Massachusetts and spent her youth in a frenzy of travel, hitchhiking, gardening, sneaking onto freight trains, writing endless letters, working on organic farms, and practicing herbalism. Her work appears in various anthologies and she blogs at https://violetcabra.dreamwidth.org/.

Nathanael Bonnell grew up in suburban Cincinnati and now lives in a little cabin in the northwoods with his partner Misty, who helps out in the running of *New Maps*. Sometimes he thinks he's escaped from his degree in anthropology unscathed, only to then discover he's written something like the two pieces in the beginning of this issue.

COLOPHON

New Maps is typeset by the editor using an ancient, temperamental program called LATEX which nevertheless produces unsurpassable results. The text font is an early digital version of Hermann Zapf's Palatino, which retains all the calligraphic warmth of the 1950s original cut that was lost in the production of the popular Linotype version. Titles are set in Sebastian Nagel's 2010 typeface Tierra Nueva, which is based on lettering from a 1562 map of the Americas; headers, drop caps, and miscellany are in Warren Chappell's classic Lydian. A cameo is made in this issue by Cagliostro, designed in 2018 by Matthew Aaron Desmond after brushwork by Oz Cooper, of Cooper Black fame.

ACKNOWLEDGEMENTS

Special thanks are due to Joel Caris, for incalculable help in getting this magazine set up; to John Michael Greer, without whom this project would never have begun; to Ava Kay and Katie Drozd, for helping me deal with the vagaries of limited solar electricity; and, always, to Misty Amber Dawn.